SW

D0440028

Eclipse

Cate Tiernan

speak
An Imprint of Penguin Group (USA) Inc.

SPEAK
Published by Penguin Group
Penguin Group (USA) Inc.,
345 Hudson Street, New York, New York 10014, U.S.A.
Penguin Books Ltd, 80 Strand, London WC2R 0RL, England
Penguin Books Australia Ltd, 250 Camberwell Road, Camberwell, Victoria 3124, Australia
Penguin Books Canada Ltd, 10 Alcorn Avenue, Toronto, Ontario, Canada M4V 3B2
Penguin Books (N.Z.) Ltd, 182-190 Wairau Road, Auckland 10, New Zealand

Published by Puffin Books,
A division of Penguin Young Readers Group, 2002

7 9 10 8 6

Cover Photography copyright 2001 Barry David Marcus
Photo-illustration by Marci Senders
Series Design by Russell Gordon

Produced by 17th Street Productions,
an Alloy, Inc. company
151 West 26th Street
New York, NY 10001

17th Street Productions and associated logos
are trademarks and/or registered trademarks of Alloy, Inc.

ISBN 0-14-230110-8

Printed in the United States of America

To Stephanie Lane, with gratitude

1.
Morgan

><"And then the hand of God swept away the
heathen witches, and their village was leveled
and burned to the ground. This I saw with my
own eyes."
—Susanna Garvey, Cumberland, England, from
A Brief Colloquial History of Cumberland,
Thomas Franklinton, 1715><

"Oh, please. Will you two stop already? This is disgusting," I teased.

On Ethan Sharp's front step Bree Warren and Robbie Gurevitch tried to disentangle themselves from their lip-to-lip suction lock. Robbie gave a little cough.

"Hey, Morgan." He stood off to one side, trying to act casual—hard to do when you're flushed and breathing hard. It was still a tiny bit of a novelty to see Robbie and Bree, my best friends from childhood, in a romantic relationship. I loved it.

"Perfect timing, Sister Mary Morgan," said Bree, pushing a hand through her minky dark hair. But she grinned at me, and I smiled back. Robbie rang Ethan's doorbell.

Ethan opened the door almost immediately. Two yipping Pomeranians bounced at his feet. "Down," he said, pushing them gently with his foot as he smiled at us. "Come on in. Most everyone's here. Still waiting on a couple. Down!" he said again. "Brandy! Kahlua! Down! Okay, you're going in the bedroom."

We entered Ethan's small brick ranch house and saw Sharon Goodfine, Ethan's girlfriend, pushing furniture back against the wall. Ethan disappeared down the hall, snapping his fingers so the dogs would follow him. Robbie went to help Sharon, and Bree and I took off our jackets and threw them on an armchair with several others.

"You two look like you're getting along," I said brightly.

"Yeah," Bree admitted. "I'm still waiting for him to figure out who the real me is and then dump me."

I shook my head. "He's loved you for a long time and seen you go through a lot. He's going to be harder to shake off than that."

Bree nodded, her gaze wandering till it fixed on Robbie. I looked around, mentally taking attendance for the circle. Our regular Saturday night circles had been different lately because Hunter had been in Canada. He'd returned a few days ago and sent my emotions into an uproar with two bits of news: one, that he'd kissed another woman in Canada, which was bad enough, and two, that he'd found a book—written by one of my ancestors—that recounted the creation of the dark wave. Learning that my soul mate had been attracted to someone else *and* that I was descended from the woman who created one of the most destructive forces imaginable had left me devastated and confused. I felt a little better now, more confident in Hunter's love and in my ability to choose to do only good magick, but both of these revelations still weighed heavily on my mind.

Hunter would be here tonight. He hadn't arrived yet, because I would have felt him. My witchy short-range sensors would have told me.

Twenty minutes later everyone in our coven, Kithic, was there, except for Hunter's cousin, Sky Eventide. She was in England recovering from a failed romance, and I couldn't help glancing across the circle at the source of her pain, Raven Meltzer. As usual, Raven had dressed for attention, wearing a red satin corset from the forties, complete with cone boobs and garters, which held up fishnet stockings marred by large, gaping holes. Men's camouflage fatigues, hacked off to make shorts, completed the outfit, along with the motorcycle boots on her feet.

"Right, then, everyone," Hunter said in that English accent that made me wild. "Let's begin."

"Welcome back, Hunter," said Jenna Ruiz.

"Yeah, welcome back," said Simon Bakehouse, Jenna's boyfriend.

"It's good to be back," Hunter said, meeting my eyes. It was like being zapped by static electricity.

Hunter Niall. The love of my life. He was tall, thin, impossibly blond, and two years older than me. Besides having the English accent that I could listen to all day, he was brave, a strong blood witch, and knew more about magick and Wicca than I could imagine learning, despite my dedication to it. He had just gotten back from two weeks in Canada, where he had found his father, Daniel. And where he had met someone named Justine Courceau. Finding out that he had kissed her had been one of the hardest things I'd ever learned. I'd for-given him—I believed that he loved me and hadn't meant to hurt me—but I didn't think I'd ever be able to forget.

Ethan's living room was carpeted, so Hunter had used sidewalk chalk to draw a perfect circle. The eleven of us stepped inside it; then Hunter closed it with a chalk line. He took four brass goblets and placed them at east, south, west, and north. One held dirt, to symbolize earth. Another held water, and a candle burned in the third: water and fire. The last cup held a cone of smoldering incense to represent air. When these were in place, he looked up and smiled at us. "Did you all enjoy Bethany Malone's circles while I was away?"

"She was pretty cool," Raven said.

"She was really nice, in a different way," Simon agreed. "There's a difference in how you make a circle and how she did."

I nodded. "That's true. And I liked all the healing stuff she taught us." An understatement. I was now taking private les-sons from Bethany, focusing almost exclusively on healing. Giving my Wicca studies this focus seemed to have helped the rest of my life come into focus, too.

"Good," said Hunter. "Maybe we'll have her back as a guest circle leader sometime."

Some of us grinned, and Hunter went on. "Now, is there any circle business we need to take care of before we start? Where are we meeting next week?"

"We can have it at my house," said Thalia Cutter.

After that, there was no more Kithic business, so Hunter cast our circle, dedicated it to the Goddess, and invoked the God and the Goddess to hear us.

"Now let's raise our power," said Hunter. "And while

our power is high, we can each think about the meaning of rebirth, of spring, about how we can each strive to, in a sense, re-create our lives each spring."

We joined hands—I was between Matt Adler and Sharon. This time Hunter began with a power chant, and we all added our voices to it as we felt ready. The ancient Gaelic words seemed to float above us, weaving a circle of power above our heads. Hunter's voice was strong and sure, and in another minute I began to feel the incredible lightening of my heart that told me I had connected with the Goddess. It wasn't like she spoke to me—but when I made a real connection to magick, the magick that exists everywhere, my worries dropped away. Pure, unquestioning joy filled my heart and my mind, and I felt a rush of love for everyone in my circle—even me—and everyone outside of my circle. It was this connection that made coming back to magick so necessary for me. It was question and answer, reason and instinct, need and fulfillment all at the same time.

Hands locked, we circled deasil around the room, our feet moving faster and faster as smiles lit our faces. Rebirth, I thought with wonder. Re-create my life. Begin anew. The quickening of life. These concepts seemed full of promise and hope, and I knew my exploration of them would be joyous and exciting.

"Morgan."

With zero warning my birth father, Ciaran MacEwan, was standing in front of me. My hands ripped away from Matt's and Sharon's, and my feet stumbled on the blue carpet.

I stared at him, my eyes widening with fear and shock. In a moment I realized that he was an image in front of me, not the real person. But a complete, realistic image, shimmering gently, as if with heat.

"Morgan," he said again, his Scottish accent coming through. His brownish hazel eyes, exactly like mine, examined me.

"What do you want?" I whispered. All I could see was him; my circle, the room, my friends had faded out of sight, replaced by this glowing image of my father, the man who had burned my mother to death more than sixteen years ago.

"I know you put the watch sigil on me," he said softly, and fear clenched my stomach. "But I forgive you."

The last time I had seen Ciaran, we had shape-shifted together. At the council's request, I had traced a watch sigil onto him so that council members could track Ciaran's movements and eventually take him into custody. It had been a betrayal of him, but the risk had outweighed the danger of the deeds he would commit if left free. My birth father was one of the most evil witches in existence. He had murdered scores of people, including my birth mother, Maeve Riordan, as well as the lover she had known from childhood. I had chosen to betray Ciaran. I had chosen good over evil.

"I've . . . dismantled the watch sigil," Ciaran went on, and my knees almost buckled. "It was beautifully done, Morgan. So subtle, so elegant, yet so powerful." He shook his head admiringly. "Your powers . . ."

Oh, Goddess, I thought in panic. I hadn't realized the watch sigil could be *undone*.

"Of course, I was unhappy that you chose to betray me to the council jackals," Ciaran said dryly. "My own daughter. My favored one. But I do forgive you. And it's gone now— they have no idea where I am." He gave a mischievous chuckle, making him appear younger than his early forties. "But I'm coming to see you, daughter. I have some questions for you."

His image faded quickly. Blinking, I felt like a wall I had been leaning against had suddenly been taken away. There was a split second of seeing the members of Kithic staring at me in concern; then everything went fuzzy, and I felt myself fall.

"Stay still." Hunter's reassuring voice made me quit trying to sit up. My eyes opened, then shut again—everything looked too bright.

"What happened?" I murmured.

"I was hoping you could tell me," said Hunter. He gently lifted my head and rested it on his crossed legs. "You just stopped dead in the middle of our power chant and turned as white as a sheet of paper. You said, 'What do you want?' and stared at nothing. Then you keeled over."

Just like that, it all came back with a sickening rush. "It was Ciaran," I said softly, looking up at Hunter. Above me, his green eyes narrowed.

"What happened?" he asked, almost fiercely. But I knew his anger wasn't directed at me.

I struggled to sit up, feeling my elbow aching where I must have hit it. The rest of the coven was gathered around, looking at me in concern. Then Bree knelt close to me, holding out a glass of water.

"Thanks," I said gratefully. I took it and sipped, and felt a bit stronger.

"What happened?" Bree asked also, her dark eyes worried.

"It was Ciaran MacEwan," I explained more loudly. "I

just—suddenly had a vision of Ciaran. And then I fainted."

That was all I wanted to say in front of everyone, and Hunter must have understood because he said, "I think perhaps we should call it a night." He put his arm around my shoulders and helped me stand up. "It would be hard to recapture the energy, anyway."

Still looking concerned, the members of Kithic started pulling on their jackets.

"Do you want me to follow you home?" Robbie asked. "Or drive you?"

I smiled at him. After Bree, Robbie had been my best friend since grade school. "No thanks," I said. "I'll be okay."

"I'll make sure she gets home," said Hunter.

We said good-bye to Ethan and Sharon, who decided to stay, and walked out into the brisk late winter evening. I breathed in the damp night air, trying to detect the first hint of spring. The change of seasons would do a lot for me. It had been a long, hard winter.

I stood next to my beloved white whale of a car, Das Boot, and rubbed my hands on my arms. I cast my senses but picked up nothing. "Hunter, Ciaran said he's taken off the watch sigil and that he knows I put it on him."

"Bloody hell," Hunter breathed.

"Yeah. Let's go to your place." I felt nervous, as if my father would leap out at me from behind Ethan's holly bush.

Hunter agreed and followed me in his own car to his house. I would feel safer there—it was a blood witch's house, spelled, protected, and familiar. I almost ran inside.

The overheated living room felt like a haven. Automatically I cast my senses again and felt Daniel Niall, Hunter's father, in the kitchen. I tried not to let Hunter see my disappointment. Until three weeks ago, Hunter hadn't seen his parents in eleven years. They had been in hiding from Ciaran and his coven, Amyranth. Though Hunter's mom had died before he'd been able to see her, his father was still alive, and the danger seemed to be gone. Things had gotten pretty bad for Mr. Niall in Canada, and Hunter's trip had ended with Hunter's bringing his father home to live with him. Mr. Niall was staying in Sky's room until she came back. If she ever did.

"Sit down," Hunter said. "I'll get you some tea." He headed to the kitchen, and soon I heard murmured voices.

The truth was, I couldn't help it—I didn't like Mr. Niall. I had been so excited to meet Hunter's father, who I'd heard so much about, who I knew meant so much to Hunter. But I'd been shocked by his appearance—he looked like a homeless person, all bones and pale skin, mussed gray hair, eyes that looked half crazy. Still, I had put on my best manners, smiling and shaking hands—and he had reacted to me as if I were a gift his cat had left on the doorstep. He wasn't mean, exactly—just standoffish and reserved. I wasn't looking forward to seeing him again.

Hunter was soon back. "Drink this," he said, holding out a small glass with an inch of dark amber liquid in it. I sniffed it. "It's sherry," he explained. "Just a tiny bit. For medicinal purposes."

I sipped it hesitantly. It didn't really ring my bells, but after it was down, I felt a bit warmer and more able to deal. Then Hunter handed me a cup of tea, and I could sense that he'd added herbs and also spelled it to be healing and soothing. It was very convenient, having a witch for a boyfriend.

"Now," said Hunter, sitting next to me on the couch, so I felt his leg warm against mine. "Tell me everything."

Feeling safer and less freaked, and becoming more and more aware of his body next to mine, I told him everything about my vision that I could remember.

"Bloody hell," Hunter said again.

The kitchen door swung open, and Daniel Niall came out, carrying a plate with a sandwich on it. He saw me on the couch and gave me a tight little nod.

"Hi, Mr. Niall," I said, trying to sound friendly.

"So what did she say?" Hunter asked his father. Mr. Niall paused at the bottom of the steps, looking pained, as if Hunter had prevented him from making a clean escape.

"She said she'd like to," Daniel said. "And her school has a break soon."

"Da was talking to my sister, Alwyn," Hunter explained. "We're trying to get her to come visit."

I knew Alwyn was now sixteen and an initiated witch. "Oh, that would be great," I said. "I'd like to meet her."

Daniel nodded again briefly and headed upstairs. I sighed, unsure if I should mention my unease to Hunter. Did Mr. Niall only treat me as he did because I was related to Ciaran? I mean, parents *always* like me. I'm a math nerd, I'm not flashy, and I don't drink or do drugs—I'm still a virgin, for God's sake! Not that I wanted to be reminded about that. But I look like I have "future librarian" stamped on my forehead. What else could Mr. Niall have against me?

"Is he settling in better?" I asked tactfully once he had gone upstairs.

Hunter shrugged ruefully. "More or less. Mostly he's

been reading Rose's diary." He was referring to Rose MacEwan, the witch who was responsible for creating the dark wave: an incredibly destructive spell that can pretty much take out a whole town and everyone in it. It didn't thrill me that a blood relative had created such a thing, but she had the same last name as Ciaran, she was Woodbane—sounded like family to me. I shuddered momentarily, thinking about her. Her story had seemed so real to me—I could almost see myself reacting the same way. It frightened me to think that such unimaginable destruction ran in my blood.

Weirdly enough, Mr. Niall had found Rose's diary in Canada, at the house of that witch, Justine Courceau. We had all read it, and then Mr. Niall had taken it back. "Da hopes that he'll find clues about how to create a spell to disband a dark wave."

"I didn't know that was possible. Goddess—if we never had to worry about it, it would be incredible. I hope he can do it." I shook my head in wonder.

"Look," Hunter said, "maybe we should scry right now, see if we can get a handle on where Ciaran is. Do you feel up to it?" He gently brushed my long hair over my shoulder. I had recently lopped off about six inches, and now it hung to the middle of my back.

"Yeah," I said, frowning. "Maybe we should. I keep feeling like he's going to drop down from the ceiling, like a spider." I followed Hunter into the large circle room, next to the dining room.

The circle room at Hunter's had once been a double parlor. Now it was a long, bare rectangle, scented with herbs and candles. There was a wood-burning stove, and in front of it Hunter made a small circle on the floor, big enough for the two of us. We sat cross-legged inside it, facing each other, our knees touching. Thoughts flew through my head as Hunter took out a large, smooth piece of obsidian: his scrying stone.

Gently we each put two fingers on the stone's edges and closed our eyes. This was where you cleared your mind and concentrated, opening yourself to what the stone wants to tell you. But all I could think about was Ciaran coming back for me, how much he scared me even as I felt oddly drawn to him. And Hunter—he wanted Hunter dead. Hunter, who was a beautiful mosaic of contradictions: strong, but infinitely gentle. Kind, but also ruthless and unforgiving when confronted by those who practiced dark magick—like Cal Blaire and Selene Belltower. I had seen Hunter flushed with desire and white-faced with anger and pain. He was my love.

"Morgan?"

"Sorry," I said.

"We don't have to do this," he offered.

"No, no, I need to." I closed my eyes again and this time, determinedly shutting out all other thoughts, I sank successfully into a deep meditation. Slowly I opened my eyes to see the smooth plane of the obsidian beneath my fingers. Lightly I murmured,

> *"Show me now what I should see,*
> *What was past or what will be.*
> *The stream of time will start to slow;*
> *Show me where I need to go."*

Hunter muttered the same words after me, and then there was silence as I focused my gaze on the stone. Minutes went by, yet the stone's face remained unchanged. It was odd—scrying is always unpredictable, but I usually got a better result than this.

Consciously I let my mind sink deeper into meditation. Everything around me faded out as I concentrated on the stone. My breathing was slow and deliberate, my chest barely moving. I no longer felt my fingers on the stone, my butt on the hard floor, my knees touching Hunter's.

The stone was black, blank. Or . . . looking closer, could I detect the barest, rounded outlines of—what? I looked at the stone so intently, I felt like I had fallen into a well of obsidian, surrounded by cold, hard blackness. Slowly I became aware of movement within the stone—that I *was* getting a scried vision. A vision of billowing, black, choking smoke.

"The blackness *is* the vision," I murmured. "Do you see the huge cloud of smoke?"

"Not clearly. Is it from a fire?"

I shook my head. "I can't see a fire. Just billows of black, choking smoke." An image of my birth mother, who had been killed by fire, came to me, and I frowned. What did it mean? Was this an image of the future? Was this directed at me? Did it mean I would suffer the same fate as Maeve, at Ciaran's hands?

For five more minutes I stared at the smoke, willing it to clear, to dissipate, to show me what was behind it. But I saw nothing more, and finally, my eyes stinging, I shook my head and sat back.

"I don't know what that was about," I told Hunter in frustration. "I didn't get anything besides smoke."

"It was a dark wave," Hunter said quietly.

"What?" I felt my back stiffen with tension. "What do you mean? Was this a prediction of a dark wave? It seemed to be about *me*." I got to my feet, feeling upset. "Is a dark wave coming for *me*?"

"We don't know for sure—you know scrying can be unpredictable," Hunter said, trying to comfort me.

"Yeah, and you know that almost every image I've ever seen scrying has come true," I said, rubbing my arms with my hands. I felt nervous and frightened, the way I'd felt as a kid, playing with a Ouija board, when it had moved on its own.

"I'll follow you home," Hunter said, and I nodded. Another downside of Mr. Niall living with him was that Hunter and I had no privacy anymore. It was one thing to be alone in Hunter's room when Sky was around, but there was no way I felt comfortable with his father in the next room. I felt depressed as I got into my jacket. Hunter and I really needed time alone to talk, to be together, to hold each other.

"Will you be okay at home?" he asked as we walked outside.

I thought. "Yeah. My house is protected out the wazoo."

"Still, I reckon it wouldn't hurt to add another layer of spells."

At my house, though we were both exhausted, Hunter and I made the rounds and added to or increased the protective powers of the spells on my house, on Das Boot, and on my parents' cars. When we were done, I felt drained.

"Go on inside," Hunter said. "Get some sleep. These spells are strong. But don't hesitate to call me if you sense anything odd."

I smiled and leaned against the front door, exhausted, wanting to be safely inside yet reluctant to leave Hunter. He came up the steps and I went into his arms, resting my head against his chest and feeling amazed at how, once again, he had seemed to read my mind.

"It'll be okay, my love," he said against my hair. One strong hand stroked my back soothingly while the other held me closely to him.

"I'm tired of it all," I said, suddenly feeling close to tears.

"I know. We haven't had a break. Listen, tomorrow why don't we go to Practical Magick, see Alyce? That'll be nice and normal."

I smiled at his idea of nice and normal: two blood witches going to an occult bookstore.

"Sounds good," I said. Then I lifted my face to his and was at once lost in the heady pleasure of kissing him, his warm lips against mine, the cool night air surrounding us, our bodies pressed together, magick sparking. Oh, yes, I thought. Yes. More of this.

"What's wrong?" I asked the next afternoon. Ever since Hunter had picked me up, he'd seemed edgy and distracted.

He drummed his fingers on the steering wheel. "I've been trying to reach the council for news on Ciaran," he said. "But I haven't been able to get through to anyone—not Kennet, not Eoife. I talked to some underling who wouldn't tell me anything."

Eoife was a witch who had tried to convince me to go study with Wiccan scholars in the wilds of Scotland. I had said I needed to finish high school first.

Kennet Muir was Hunter's mentor in the council and had helped guide him through the hard process of becoming a Seeker. Hunter still spoke to him about council business, but their relationship had been permanently damaged when Hunter realized Kennet had known where his parents were in Canada and hadn't bothered to tell him. If Kennet had let Hunter in on their whereabouts earlier, Hunter might have seen his mother alive. I knew this idea was hard for him to accept. In fact, he was so hurt by Kennet's betrayal, he never even confronted him about it. "It'll never be the same between us regardless," he'd reasoned.

"Okay, so we don't know," I said, watching the old farm fields fly past the car window. After being winter brown for months, it was heartening to see tinges and flecks of green here and there. Spring was coming. No matter what.

"No. Not yet." Hunter sounded irritated. Then he seemed to make an effort to cheer up. Reaching out one hand, he interlaced his fingers in mine and smiled at me. "It's good to spend time with you. I missed you so much when I was in Canada."

"I missed you, too." Once again exercising my gift for understatement. Then, taking a breath, I decided to bring up a sensitive subject. "Hunter—I've been wondering about your dad. I mean, he knows I'm not in league with Ciaran, right? He knows Ciaran tried to kill me, doesn't he?"

Hunter tugged at the neck of his sweater, pretending to not understand me. "He just needs more time."

Great. I looked out the window again.

"Is it Rose?" I asked suddenly, turning back to Hunter. "Is it because I'm a descendant of the witch who created the dark wave? I mean, he was running from the dark wave for eleven years." Eleven years, while Hunter was separated from his parents, thinking they'd abandoned him and his brother and sister. My stomach plummeted as I realized yet again how many horrible things my blood relatives were responsible for.

Hunter glanced over at me, taking his eyes off the road, and in that quick glance I caught a world of reassurance. "He just needs to get to know you, Morgan. You are not your ancestors. I know that."

I sighed, watching the bare trees pass overhead. If only I could convince *myself*.

Red Kill, the town where Practical Magick was, came into view slowly, the farm fields giving way to suburban lawns, then more streets and actual neighborhoods. Hunter turned down Main Street and drove almost to its end, where the small building that housed Practical Magick stood. He parked, but I made no move to get out of the car.

"It's just, I want your father to like me," I said, feeling self-conscious. "And I don't want to come between you and your dad. I don't want you to have to choose." I looked down at my hands, which were twisting nervously in my lap. I forced them to be still on my jeans.

"Goddess," Hunter muttered, leaning over the gearbox toward me. He took my chin in his hand and looked intently into my eyes. His were the color of olivine, a clear, deep green. "I won't need to choose. Like I said, Da just needs more time. He knows how much I love you. He just needs to get used to the idea."

I sighed and nodded. Hunter touched my cheek briefly, and then we opened the doors, climbed out, and headed for the store.

"Morgan, Hunter! Good to see you." Alyce Fernbrake waved us in from the back of the store. "I haven't seen either of you in a while. Hunter, I want to hear all about Canada. I couldn't believe your news. Wait—I'll fix tea."

We threaded our way through the scented, crowded store: my home away from home. Alyce disappeared into the small back room, separated from the main room by a tattered orange curtain. Her assistant, Finn Foster, nodded at Hunter with reserve: Many witches didn't trust Seekers. "'Lo, Morgan," he said. "Have you heard Alyce's news? The shop next door is moving to a bigger location. Alyce is going to move to that space and make Practical Magick almost twice as big."

My eyebrows rose. "The dry cleaners are moving? What about her debt to Stuart Afton? Can she afford to lose their rent?"

Alyce bustled back with three mugs. "Well, fortunately, my business has been getting better and better the last couple of months. The real estate market is good enough that if I move into the store next door, I can rent this space for almost as much as the dry cleaners paid. And we'll just have to keep our fingers crossed that our increased sales will make up for the rest. It's a gamble, but I think it will be worth it in the end." She smiled.

"Congratulations," Hunter said, taking his mug. "It would be fantastic if the shop were bigger."

Alyce nodded, looking pleased. "It's going to be a lot of work," she said, "and I really don't know when I'll have the time. But I think the business could support the extra room. I would love to expand what I carry." She gestured to a pile of about five paper grocery bags, each packed with old-looking books. "I buy stuff at yard sales, estate sales, things that interest me, but I don't really have the space to put them out. You should see what I have in storage. But now I want to hear about you. It's amazing that your father has come to live with you."

Hunter nodded, and the two of them drifted over to the checkout counter, where Alyce propped herself on a stool and Hunter leaned against the lighted case. I went over to the bags of old books and started poking around, sure that Alyce wouldn't mind. I decided to sort them for her and started making piles of nonoccult books and some history books. Then, in the second bag, I found some titles about Wicca, the history of the Sabbats, some spell-crafting guides, some astrology charts. Hunter and Alyce were still chatting, Alyce occasionally taking a break to wait on customers. Finn was reorganizing the essential oils shelves, and everything around me smelled like cloves and vanilla and roses.

Now I was surrounded by stacks, and in the fifth bag I found some interesting older books about weatherworking and animal magick. There were a couple of old Books of Shadows, too, handwritten, filled with writing and diagrams. One looked quite old: the writing was spiky, from a fountain pen, and the pages were deep tan with age. Another book looked newer and also less interesting: fewer drawings and long periods of no writing. There was another BOS, in a green-cloth-bound diary. It looked much newer and less romantic than the others, but I flipped through it. It was written by a witch during the seventies! So cool. Most recent Books of Shadows are still in the possession of their owners. This was unusual, and I started reading it.

"Morgan, shall we?" Hunter asked a few minutes later.

I nodded. "I sorted your books," I told Alyce, gesturing to my piles.

"Oh, how nice!" she said, clasping her hands together. She's shorter than I am and rounded in an old-fashioned womanly way. She looked like a youngish grandmother from a fairy-tale book, all in gray and lavender and purple.

"This one is great," I said, holding up the one I'd been reading. "It's from the seventies. Are you going to sell these books? Maybe I could buy it."

"Oh, please." Alyce waved her hands at me. "Take it, it's yours. Consider it payment for sorting all these bags."

"Thanks," I said, smiling. "I appreciate it. Thanks a lot."

"Come back soon," she said.

In the car Hunter and I looked at each other. I felt a tiny smile cross my lips.

"I think I need to work on convincing you of my undying love," Hunter said mischievously, reading my expression. "Let's see. I could cast a spell that would write your name in the clouds. Or I could take you out for a nice meal—or we could go to my house and fool around on my bed. You know, as practice before we do the real thing."

"Is your dad at your house?" I asked. Hunter and I had both wanted to make love for what seemed like a very long time. But the last time it came up, right before he left for Canada, Hunter had decided that we should wait. It was important to both of us for it to be just right—but who knew when that would ever happen?

"No. Today's he's at Bethany's," said Hunter. "She's been doing some deep healing work with him."

My eyes lit up. "Oh, yeah, let's go to your house!"

2.
Alisa

>< "The barrier between the world and the netherworld is both stronger and weaker than we ken. Strong in that it never breaches by itself, come earthquakes, floods, or famine. Weak in that one witch with a spell can rend it, allowing the passage of things unnamable."
—Mariska Svenson, Bodø, Norway, 1873 ><

"It's okay, Alisa," said my friend Mary K. Rowlands on Monday afternoon. "You're not a guy. You can come in."

I laughed and followed her into the living room. Both of Mary K.'s parents worked, and she and her sister, Morgan, weren't allowed to have boys over when their parents weren't there. It was so funny—almost antique. But her folks are really Catholic and keep Mary K. and Morgan on pretty tight leashes.

"Let's hang in the kitchen," Mary K. called over her shoulder.

"That's where the food is," I agreed.

Everything about the Rowlandses' house looks like it got frozen in about 1985. The living room is done in hunter green plaids with maroon accents. The kitchen is dusty blue and dusty pink, with a goose theme. It's corny, but oddly comforting. Now that my evil stepmother-to-be was madly redecorating the house I shared with my dad, I really appreciated anything familiar.

I dumped my messenger bag on the wood-grained Formica table while Mary K. rustled through the fridge and the pantry. She surfaced with a couple of bottles of Frappaccino, some apples, and a big bag of peanut M&M's.

I nodded my approval. "I see you've covered all the major food groups."

She grinned. "We aim to please."

We settled down at the kitchen table with our food and our textbooks open. I had been going to Mary K.'s pretty often after school lately—I guess to avoid going home—and Mary K. was really cool. A good friend. She seemed so normal and kind of reassuring somehow, especially compared to Morgan. Morgan had done a lot to weird me out in the past. I still wasn't sure what to make of her.

"Alisa?" Mary K. said, twirling a strand of hair around one finger as she frowned at her math book. "Do you have any idea what the difference is between real and natural numbers?"

"No," I said, and took a swig of Frappaccino. "Hey, did Mark ask you out for Friday?"

"No," she said, looking disappointed. She'd been crushing on Mark Chambers for weeks now, but though he was really nice to her, he didn't seem to be picking up on her "date me" vibes. "But it's only Monday. Maybe I could ask him, if he hasn't asked me by Thursday."

"You go, Mary K. Fight the system." I smiled, encouraging

her. Then I sighed, thinking about my own romantic possibilities. "God, I wish I had a crush on someone. Or someone had a crush on me. Anything to break up the delirious joy of being around my dad and Hilary."

Mary K. made a sympathetic face. "How's the Hiliminator?"

I shrugged, my shoulders rising and falling dramatically. "Well, she's still with us," I reported dryly, and Mary K. laughed. My dad's pregnant girlfriend had recently moved into our house, and now she was already pooching out in front, before they were actually getting hitched. I couldn't believe my straitlaced, ultraconservative dad had gotten himself into this nightmare. It was like living with a couple of strangers. "But she's quit barfing, which is good. Every time I had to listen to her hurl, I got the dry heaves."

"Maybe the baby will be incredibly cute, and you'll be a great big sister, and when she grows up, you guys will be really close," Mary K. suggested. She couldn't help it: she was born to pour sunshine on other people. It was one of the things I loved about her.

"Yeah," I allowed. "*Or* maybe it'll be a boy, and when I'm forced to change his diaper, he'll pee right in my face."

"Oh, gross!" Mary K. shrieked, and we both started laughing. "Alisa, that is so, so gross. If he ever does that, do *not* tell me about it."

"Anyway," I said with a giggle, "I've been suggesting names. If it's a girl, Alisa Junior. If it's a boy, Aliso."

We were still laughing about that one when the back door opened and Morgan came in. She smiled when she saw us, and I made myself smile back. It wasn't that I didn't like Morgan. It was mostly that I thought she was kind of dangerous—even though she could be nice and thoughtful sometimes. Morgan is a witch, a real witch. Some kids around here are—they call themselves blood witches because they're born to it, like having blue eyes or bad skin. Mary K. isn't, because though they are sisters, Morgan was adopted.

Morgan and some other kids from my high school (Mary K. is a freshman, I'm a sophomore, and Morgan is a junior) even have their own coven, called Kithic. I had been to circles with Kithic and had thought they were so—incredible. Special. Natural, somehow. But I had quit going a while back when Morgan had started making scary things happen, like breaking things without touching them. Like that girl in *Carrie*. And I saw her make crackling blue energy on her hand once. Mary K. had even told me (in total secret) that she thought Morgan had done something magicky when their aunt's girlfriend had cracked her head open at an ice rink. Mary K. said that Paula had looked like she was really hurt, and everyone was freaking, but Morgan put her hands on her and *fixed* her. I mean, how scary is that? It wasn't anything I wanted to be around.

"Youngsters," Morgan greeted us with a snobby nod. But she was just kidding—she and Mary K. get along really well.

"You know, Morgan," Mary K. said with an innocent expression, "I'm the same age younger than *you* as you are from *Hunter*. Isn't that funny?" No one can look more wide-eyed and who-me? than Mary K.

Morgan dropped her backpack on the kitchen table with a heavy thud and gave Mary K. a poisonous look—then they both laughed. I wished I had a sister—no, not one *fifteen* years younger than me, but a real one, who I could talk to and hang out with, who could join forces with me against my wicked stepmonster-to-be.

"Studying, are we?" Morgan asked.

"We are," said Mary K. "Trying to, at least."

Morgan reached into the fridge and grabbed a Diet Coke. She popped the top and drank, leaning against the counter. Hilary had banished sodas from our house—we were all supposed to eat more healthily than that—and I found myself watching Morgan with envy. I almost wanted to have a soda here just because I could, even though I hate Diet Coke. Morgan set down the can, wiped her mouth on her sleeve, and breathed out. She'd gotten her fix.

"You know, watching you do that makes me feel . . . *tainted* somehow," Mary K. observed, and Morgan laughed again.

"Nature's perfect food," she said, then got some hamburger out of the fridge and pulled out a big frying pan. When the fridge door shut again, a small gray cat streaked into the room and stood around mewing.

"He heard the fridge," Mary K. said.

"Hey, Dag, sweetie," Morgan said, bending down to give him a tiny bit of hamburger. The kitten mewed loudly again, then chowed down, purring hard.

"Are we having tacos?" Mary K. asked.

"Burritos." Morgan opened the package and dumped the meat into the pan.

"The Hiliminator can't stand the smell of meat lately," I said, feeling a thin new layer of irritation settle over me. "Or fried food. Or spicy food. It makes her sick. We're down to like three acceptable food items at my house: bread, rice, and crackers."

Morgan nodded as sympathetically as Mary K. had. "You can come over here and eat real food whenever you want."

"Thanks," I said. "So you're going to ask Mark out?" I asked Mary K.

"I guess," said Mary K.

"He's cute," said Morgan. She put a cutting board on the table, elbowing her backpack out of the way. The top hadn't been fastened tight, and a couple of books and notebooks spilled out. I glanced at them as she pushed the bag aside and set a block of cheddar cheese on the board, along with a grater. "Grate," she told Mary K.

"I'm doing my homework," Mary K. pointed out.

"You're talking about cute guys. Grate."

The books in Morgan's backpack caught my eye. One was an advanced calc book; then there were two spiral notebooks with doodles on the covers, and another, green-covered book, like an old-fashioned diary, peeped out from underneath those.

"Oh, did you notice Mom's crocuses out front?" Morgan asked, rolling up her sleeves. As usual, she looked like Morgan of the Mounties, in a plaid flannel shirt, worn jeans, and clogs. Somehow it looked okay on her. If I wore that, I would look like a truck driver.

Mary K. shook her head, busily grating. "What about 'em?"

"They're dying, dead," said Morgan. She pulled her long brown hair out of the way, braided it in back of her head, and snapped an elastic on the end. "They only started blooming last week, 'cause it's been so cold. The crocuses were up and the hyacinths were starting to poke out—now they're all brown lumps."

"It hasn't frozen lately, has it?" Mary K. asked.

Morgan shook her head. "Mom's going to be bummed when she sees it. Maybe they have some kind of disease." She started slicing a head of lettuce, making long strips suitable for burritoing.

"Hmmm," said Mary K.

I was listening to all this with only one ear because I just couldn't stop looking at Morgan's books. Not books, really. Book. It was freaky, but I was just dying to know what that green book was. I couldn't think about anything else until I figured it out. I didn't even know I was reaching for it when I finally realized Mary K. had been saying, "Alisa? Alisa?"

"Oh, what? Sorry," I said as Morgan turned around from the stove.

"I was saying that if you liked someone, too, then maybe we could all go out, the four of us, and then it wouldn't be so weird for me and Mark," she repeated.

"Oh." The words barely even registered. All I could think was green book, green book, green book. What was *wrong* with me? I tried to shake it off. "Um, well, I don't really like anyone. And no one likes me," I admitted. "I mean, *people* like me, but no guys specifically like me."

Mary K. frowned. "Why not? You're such a cutie."

I laughed. I knew I wasn't hideous—my dad is Hispanic, and I have his dark eyes and olive skin. My mom was Anglo, so my hair is a honey-streaked brown. I'm kind of different looking, but I don't make babies scream. But so far my sophomore year at Widow's Vale High had been a total bust, guys-wise. "I don't know."

"Morgan, do you know any guys, like friends of friends, that maybe we could set something up with?" Mary K. went on, and my mind and eyes wandered again to the stupid green book. What was it? I wanted to know. I needed to know. I shook my head silently, wondering what was going on. Why was I being so weird? It was like this crazy green book was invading my mind. Was this a temporary thing, or was it going to last? Years from now, was I going to be sitting in a padded cell somewhere, babbling, "Green book, green book, green book"? It was probably just some horrible extra-credit calc or something.

"That's a cool book," I heard Morgan say, and my head snapped up to see her and Mary K. both looking at me. I jerked back my hand, realizing with embarrassment that I had been reaching for the book again. What was *with* me? "It's a Book of Shadows," Morgan explained, glancing at Mary K., who seemed to take no notice. "I just got it today at Practical Magick."

I frowned and put both my hands in my lap. Magick. So it was a witch book. Well, that oughta cure me. I'd had enough freaky encounters with witchy things—and witchy people.

"Oh, dang!" Morgan said, turning around with irritation. "I forgot the stupid flavor packet! Well, I'm not going back to the store."

As she stood, frowning, the refrigerator door swung open. A glass butter dish, complete with butter, crashed to the ground, shattering. We all stared at it.

"Was that propped on something in there?" Mary K. asked.

"It was in the butter thing on the door," Morgan said, frowning even more.

I jumped up almost without realizing it. Oh, God, not again, I thought as horror filled my veins. Morgan just could not control her powers! She was a walking hazard! I had to get away from her. I *hated* this kind of stuff. True, this was just a broken butter dish, but I'd seen far worse happen before. Who knew what would happen next? What if she made *knives* start flying around or something?

"Did you not close the door?" Mary K. persisted. Morgan sighed and tiptoed to the broom closet, taking out a broom and a dustpan. Morgan with a broom, I thought. How appropriate.

"No, I closed it." Morgan sounded fed up. "I don't know what happened."

Uh-huh. And my mom is Queen Elizabeth, I thought.

Morgan scowled down at the broken dish as if she could reconstruct it with her eyes and make it all rush backward and mend itself, like in the movies. Actually, maybe she could. I didn't know.

"I didn't—" she began, and then her head lifted. "Hunter," she said. Wiping her hands on a kitchen towel, she walked out the kitchen door, leaving hamburger sizzling on the stove, a broken butter dish (that *she* had broken) right there on the floor. A moment later we heard the front door open and shut.

"What about Hunter?" I said.

Mary K. looked a little uncomfortable as she used a paper towel to pick up the glass-encrusted butter and put it in the trash. "Hunter's here, I guess."

"Did you hear his car?" I didn't even know why I was asking. I knew the answer. It was Morgan, Morgan the witch, Morgan and her freaky powers. She'd heard Hunter coming with her superpowerful witchy ears.

Mary K. shrugged and began to sweep up glass. I stood up and turned off the fire under the hamburger, giving the meat a quick stir. Without meaning to, I glanced at the table and was immediately drawn again to the green book. What *was* it about that book?

3.
Morgan

><"Young Michael Orris was down to the shore, fetching seaweed for the garden. He looked up and saw a black curtain falling over the land like a sunset. Being a lad of six, he were scared and hid behind a rock. When the sun came out, he ran home to find nothing but broken stones, still smoking. Years later I heard he never made his initiation. Didn't want to be anything like a witch, not ever."
—Peg Curran, Tullamore, Ireland, 1937><

"You don't look like a happy camper," I said, crossing my arms over my chest. I'd come out without a jacket as soon as I'd felt Hunter's presence. The thing with the butter dish had totally thrown me—we'd never figured out why the weird telekinetic stuff happened. I was afraid that it might be a sign from Ciaran, just to let me know he was watching. "I'm glad you're here—something weird just happened—"

"I just came from a meeting with the council," Hunter uncharacteristically interrupted me. "Kennet flew in yesterday, which is why I couldn't get hold of him. They called me this morning."

"What was it about? Did you find out anything about Ciaran?"

"Yes." Hunter seemed tightly coiled, like a snake, and I felt anger coming off him in heated waves. He strode past my mother's crumpled crocuses and up onto the porch. "I did." He reached out to enfold me in his arms. "Apparently Ciaran dismantled the watch sigil two weeks ago. He hasn't been seen since."

I pulled back and stared at him. "Two *weeks* ago?" I choked out. Oh, Goddess. Oh, no. My father could in fact be hiding under my front porch *right now*. I went rigid with fear. He could have been watching me for almost *two weeks* now. "Goddess," I whispered. "And the council didn't share this because . . . ?"

He shook his head, looking disgusted. "They have no good reason. They said it was on a 'need to know' basis. Why they didn't think you or I needed to know is a complete mystery. I think they're just embarrassed that he's slipped through their fingers again. Obviously they should have taken him in before now and stripped his powers. But they were hoping he would lead them to other cells of Amyranth. Now he's gone."

The image of Ciaran having his powers stripped was disturbing—I'd seen it happen before, and it was horrifying. But the image of Ciaran coming after me with full powers— maybe *being* in Widow's Vale *right now*—was much, much worse. "I can't believe it," I said, feeling anger rise in me like acid. "Who the hell do they think they are? I don't need to know my own father is free? When I'm the one who put the watch sigil on him?"

Hunter nodded grimly. "Too right. I don't know what they're doing. The council was never intended to be able to act with impunity. They seem to have forgotten that, and that they have a responsibility and an obligation to the witches they represent. Not to mention their own fellow council members."

"I can't believe it," I said again. "Those *asses*. So we can assume that Ciaran is around here somewhere." I thought about it. "I haven't picked up on anything, except the vision."

"Nor I. But I think we can guess he's coming to at least talk to you, like he said."

"What should we do? What are you going to do?"

"We need to be incredibly vigilant and on guard," he said. "I'm going to demand that the council take some responsibility for once, take some real action. In the meantime, your house and car are about as protected as I know how."

I closed my eyes. I had liked Eoife, the council witch I knew the best, but I was outraged that they had bungled this so badly and hadn't bothered to tell me. Surely they knew that I would be in danger. What had they been *thinking*?

"The council—" Hunter began, then stopped abruptly, clearly as upset as I was. "It's like they're falling apart, with certain factions acting without the knowledge or approval of the others. When it was first formed, Dinara Rafferty was the head. Nowadays the whole thing is being run, and badly, by a witch named Cynthia Pratt. She doesn't seem to have a handle on anything."

"Great. So now what?"

"I don't know," he admitted. "I have to think about it. But maybe we should try scrying again, see if we can pick up on anything about Ciaran at all." He glanced over my shoulder. "Can I come in?"

My parents would be home from work soon. I had to finish getting dinner together. I glanced at my watch. "I have maybe ten minutes, max," I said. "But if my mom or dad comes home early, you'll have to get yourself out of here without them seeing."

He nodded, and I opened the front door, almost hitting Alisa, who was on her way out. She shot me a startled glance and clutched her messenger bag tighter to her chest. With a jolt I remembered the broken butter dish and sighed. Given the way Alisa was eyeing me, she thought I'd done my *Blair Witch* act. It was unfortunate that these things often seemed to happen when she was around.

"Hi, Alisa," Hunter said absently, stepping aside to let her pass. "Hope you're feeling better." Alisa had been hospitalized about a month ago for some kind of flu, but she seemed fine now.

"Thanks," Alisa muttered; then she scuttled past us on the porch and went down the stairs. I watched her for a moment; then Hunter and I entered the warmth of my house.

In my room, where the only male creatures allowed were my father and Dagda, Hunter and I sat on my woven grass rug and lit a candle. We surrounded it with protective stones: agate, jade, malachite, moonstone, olivine, a pearl, black tourmaline, a chunk of rock salt, and a pale brown topaz. We linked hands, touched knees, and looked into the candle. I knew we had only minutes, so I concentrated hard and ruthlessly shut out any extraneous thoughts. Ciaran, I thought. Ciaran. Hunter's power blended with mine, and we both focused our energy on the candle.

The glow of the candle filled my eyes until it seemed that the whole room around me was glowing. Slowly a figure began to emerge, black, from the glow. My heart quickened, and I waited for Ciaran's face to become recognizable. But when the glow faded a bit, it revealed instead a woman or a girl—her back was to me. She raised one arm and wrote sigils in the air. I didn't recognize them. I got the impression she was working magick, powerful magick, but I didn't know what kind. Who are you? I thought. Why am I seeing you? As if in answer, the girl started turning to face me. But before I saw her features, a great, rolling wave of fire swept toward her. She crumpled underneath it, and the fire swept on. I waited to see the twisted and charred body left behind, but before I could, the image winked out, as if someone had turned off a slide projector.

I sat back, disappointed and confused.

"What I saw didn't make sense," Hunter said finally, blowing out the candle.

"It didn't to me, either," I said. "I didn't see Ciaran at all—just a girl and a fire."

"What does it mean?" he asked in frustration, and then we heard a gentle tap on the door.

"Mom just pulled up," Mary K. said quietly.

Quickly I put the candle away and Hunter slipped back into his jacket. I opened my bedroom door.

"Thanks," I told my sister.

She looked at me pointedly. "I got dinner together for you. I cleaned up the broken glass. And now I've told you mom's home so your ass won't be in a sling."

"Oh, Mary K.," I said gratefully. "Thank you. I owe you one."

"You sure do," she agreed, and I followed her down the stairs.

"Be careful," I heard Hunter barely breathe in back of me, and I nodded. Then my mom was in the living room, and I went to the kitchen to finish dinner, and soon after that my dad came home. I never heard Hunter leave, but half an hour later I remembered to glance out the window, and of course his car was gone. It made me feel incredibly alone.

4.
Alisa

><"The question is, are we going to tolerate witches
who are of mixed or unknown clans? Witches
whose view of magick is contrary to what we
know and hold to be true? Why should we? Why
should a clear stream allow mud to cloud its
waters? And if we choose to keep our lines pure,
how do the other clans fit in? They don't."
—Clyda Rockpell, Albertswyth, Wales, 1964><

This is it, I thought, staring at the green book that lay before
me on my bed. This is the beginning of my complete and
total slide toward hell. Now I am a thief.

I had never stolen anything in my life, yet when I saw that
stupid green book of Morgan's, I had been taken over by my
evil twin. My *stupid* evil twin. Only the three of us were in
their kitchen. If Morgan noticed the book was gone, she'd
ask Mary K. Mary K. wouldn't know, and by a lightning-swift
process of elimination, one name would come up: Alisa Soto.
Sticky Fingers Soto. Which is why I'd pretty much avoided
both of them at school today. But neither of them had acted
funny when I'd seen them, so maybe Morgan hadn't missed
the book yet.

The only thing I had going for me was that Dad was at work, of course, and Hilary must be at her Mama Yoga class since it was Tuesday. Yay. I had no witnesses to my crime.

It was hard—no, impossible—to explain. But when I had seen that book fall out of Morgan's backpack, it was like it was *my* book that I had lost a long time ago, and here it was. So I took it back.

Just in case Hilary popped in anytime soon, I locked my bedroom door. I felt strange—maybe some of Morgan's weirdness was rubbing off on me. I almost felt like I was dreaming—watching myself do stuff without knowing why.

I ran my fingers over the cloth cover and felt a very faint tingle. I flipped open the cover, and the first thing I saw was a handwritten name. My eyes widened—it was Sarah Curtis, which was my own mother's maiden name! "Oh my God," I whispered, not believing what I was seeing. Was this why I had been so drawn to it?

I began to read. It was a diary, a journal, that Sarah started keeping in 1968, when she was fifteen, my age. Flipping through to the back, I saw that the book ended in 1971. I leaned back against my pillows and pulled my grandmother's flowery crocheted afghan over my feet. Ever since Hilary had moved in, our thermostat had been set to "Ice Age."

From the very first page I was totally hooked, but the book only got stranger. My jaw dropped by the second page, when I saw that Sarah Curtis lived in Gloucester, Massachusetts—just like my mom. How many Curtises could there be in one Massachusetts town? Maybe a lot. Maybe Curtises had lived there so long the name was really common. But if it wasn't, what did that mean? Could I be sitting here reading *my mom's* diary? It was impossible! I had gotten this book from Morgan!

Then a chill went down my spine: Morgan had said this was a witch book. My eyes opened wider, and the back of my neck tightened.

On Saturday will be the annual Blessing of the Fleet. It's funny how today people still rely on the old traditions. Mom says the fleet has been blessed every year for over a hundred years. Of course, it's the Catholics who run it and make the big show. But I know that Rôiseal always does our part as well.

I stopped for a moment. Ròiseal? The Blessing of the Fleet I had heard about—a lot of fishing communities have it every year, where the priest comes out and sprinkles holy water on the bows of the fishing boats to protect them through the year and give them luck.

Sam and I went down to Filbert's today and got some orange soda pop. Mom would kill us if she knew. Mom and her "whole food, natural food" stuff. She thinks artificial flavors and tastes are enough to dull your senses and abilities. I haven't noticed any difference.

Whoa, I thought. And I thought Hilary was bad, with her organic toilet paper. I mean, she thought sodas weren't good for you, but I didn't think she actually believed they would dull your senses. A glimmer of a memory went through my head, of my mom saying something to me, telling me a story about when she was a little girl. About how funny her mom had been about some stuff. But the memory was too vague to really remember—maybe I was getting mixed up. After all, my mom had died when I was three. This *was* an amazing coincidence, though. *If* it was a coincidence, a scared little voice inside me whispered.

I'm still trying to talk Mom and Dad into an out-of-state college. I figure I have another three years to work on them—who knows what could happen? They just don't want me mixing with people who aren't like us—like if I meet enough different people, I'll leave and not come back.

I frowned as I remembered Dad telling me about how Mom's parents hadn't wanted her to go away to college, either. Oh, God—what did this mean? This couldn't just be a coincidence. But how was it possible—God! As if mesmerized, I turned back to the book for answers.

The lilacs have been blooming for a couple of weeks now. Their scent is everywhere. When I go outside, the damp salt of the sea is overlain with their gorgeous, heavy perfume. Mom's bushes are covered with bees in ecstasy. Seeing the lilacs in bloom breaks me out of my Northeast winter blues every year. I know that warm weather is coming, that summer is almost here, that school will soon be out.

My throat felt like it was closing. Once I had brought home a little bunch of lilacs from the grocery store, and Dad had looked at them and turned pale. Later he told me that they'd been Mom's favorite flower, that she had carried them at their wedding, and that it still made him sad to see them. So I'd eightysixed the lilacs. *Oh, Mom,* I thought desperately. *What's going on?*

In the meantime, my asinine brother, Sam, is still auditioning for the world's-biggest-pain-in-the-butt award. Last week he switched all the copper plant labels in the garden around, so the chard has "carrots" written above it and the corn has "radishes." Mom almost had a fit. And twice he's taken my bike and stored it up on the widow's walk. It was a nightmare getting it down through the trapdoor, listening to him cackling in his room. But I'm getting him back—this morning I sewed the toes of all his socks together. Insert wicked laugh here.

I chuckled, feeling relief sweep through me. Thank God. This wasn't my mom. This Sarah Curtis had a brother. My mom was an only child, and Dad had said by the time he met her, she was estranged from her family and never saw them. That's so sad. It means I grew up with only one set of grandparents and cousins. None from her side. But God, what a relief to hear this woman had a brother. I had been practically shaking with dread about this witch Sarah Curtis.

Time to go. I have to practice the full moon rite that I'm supposed to do on Litha.

I turned the page.

Okay, I'm back. Mom is in the kitchen, making a healing tea for Aunt Jess. Her tonsilitis is acting up. I can't believe I have school tomorrow. I keep looking at the calendar: three more weeks till Litha. Litha and summer. Mom and I have been crafting a fertility spell for the last two months. Basically it's to make everything in the land and sea do well and multiply. A typical Rowanwand all-purpose spell. I can't wait. At Litha all of Ròiseal will be there, and it will be the first big spell I've cast in public since my initiation last Samhain.

With a thud all my sensations of fear and nervousness came back. This *couldn't* be my mom—I knew that. But someone with my mom's name had written this book. Hands trembling, I set it down.

She had come from Gloucester, Massachusetts. Like my mom.

Like my mom, she'd loved lilacs. It was too weird, too similar.

But some things didn't fit: her brother, Sam. The fact that *this* Sarah Curtis had been a Rowanwand *witch*.

Crash! I jumped about a foot in the air. My wooden jewelry box had fallen off my dresser and was lying on its side on the floor. How the hell had *that* happened?

This was all crazy. I closed the book without marking my place and went to my jewelry box. It was one of the very few things I had that had been my mom's. I picked it up and cradled it in my arms.

That Sarah Curtis had been a witch.

My mom hadn't been a witch. I searched my patchy, foggy memories. My mom, who smelled of lilacs. Her smile, her light brown hair, her laugh, the way it felt when she held me. There had been nothing about her that said witch. I didn't remember spells or chants or circles or even candles. There were two Sarah Curtises. One of them had been a witch. One of them had been my mom. Just my mom.

I took the box over to my bed, unlatched it, and dumped everything out on my comforter. My fingers brushed through the fake jewelry, the goofy pins I collected, the charm bracelet my dad had been adding to since I was six. There were a few pieces of my mom's jewelry, too: her engagement ring, with its tiny sapphire. Some pearl earrings. Even an anklet with little bells on it.

I looked at the empty box as if it would reassure me somehow. None of this could be real. There had to be some sort of explanation. A nonwitch explanation. My mom hadn't even *had* a brother.

Open me.

I hadn't heard the words—I had felt them. I stared down at the box as if it had turned into a snake. This was too creepy. But, compelled, I turned it upside down. I shook it, but nothing more came out. I opened and closed it a couple of times, looking for another latch somewhere, a hidden hinge. Nothing. Inside I ran my fingers around the lid and down the sides. Nothing. There was a small tray insert that I had dumped out onto my bed. The bottom of the box was lined with cushioned pink satin. I pressed it with my fingers, but there were no lumps or catches anywhere. I was imagining things.

Then I saw the pale pink loop of thread sticking out from one side of the cushion. I hooked my finger into it and pulled gently, and the whole cushion came up in my hand. Beneath the cushion was the wooden bottom of the box. There was a tiny catch on one side, tarnished and almost impossible to see. I poked it with one fingernail, and nothing happened. I turned the box another way and held it in my lap and pushed at the latch again.

With a tiny *snick* the bottom of the box swung upward. And I was staring at a yellowed pile of old letters, tied with a faded green ribbon.

The ribbon was tattered and practically untied itself in my hands. The letters were written on a bunch of different kinds of paper—loose-leaf, stationery, printer paper. I picked one up and unfolded it, feeling like I was watching someone else do this. From downstairs I heard the thud of the front door closing, but I ignored it and began to read.

Dear Sarah,

I'm so glad you finally contacted me. I can't believe you've been gone six whole months. It feels like years. I miss you so much. After you left, there was nothing but bad scenes, and now no one even speaks your name. It's like you died, and it makes me so sad, all the time. I'm glad to hear you're okay. I've set up a PO box over in North Heights, and you can write me there. I know Mom and Dad would flip right now if they saw a letter from you.

I better go—I'll write again soon. Take care.

Your brother, Sam.

Tap, tap. The knock on my bedroom door made me jerk.

"Allie?" Oh, *God.* Not Hilary. Not now. How many times had I told her I hated to be called Allie? A thousand? More?

"Yeah?"

"I'm home."

I had a feeling, I thought, since you're speaking to me. "Okay," I called.

"Do you want a snack? I have some dried fruit. Or maybe some yogurt?"

"Oh, no thanks, Hilary. I'm not really hungry."

Pause. "You shouldn't go too long without eating," she said. "Your blood sugar will crash."

I felt like screaming. Why was I having this conversation? My past was unraveling before my eyes, and she was going on about my freaking blood sugar!

"It's *okay*," I said, aware that some irritation had entered my voice. "I'll deal with my blood sugar."

Silence. Then her footsteps retreating down the hall. I sighed. No doubt I would hear about that later. For some reason, neither Hilary nor Dad could understand why I might have some trouble getting used to having his pregnant, twenty-five-year-old girlfriend living with us.

I shuffled the letters randomly and picked up another one.

Dear Sarah,

I'm sorry I couldn't make the wedding. You know October is one of our busiest times. I have to tell you: You're my sister, and I love you, but I can't help feeling disappointed that you married an outsider. I know you *turned your back on your magick, but can you turn your back on your entire heritage? What if you, by some miracle, have a child with this outsider? Can you stand to not raise the child Rowanwand? I don't get it.*

A few paragraphs down it was signed *Sam*.

I felt hot and a little dizzy. The truth kept trying to break into my consciousness, but I held it back. Just one more letter.

Dear Sarah,

Blessings on your good news. Since you moved to Texas, I've been worried about you. It seems so far away. I hope you and my new niece, Alisa, will be happy there. Dad has been sick again this spring—his heart—but no one thinks it's as serious as it was two years ago. I'll keep you posted.

The letter fluttered from my fingers like an ungainly butterfly. Oh, God. Oh, God. I swallowed convulsively, pressing my hand to my mouth. I had been born in Texas. My name was Alisa. Reality crashed down on me like a breaker at the shore, and like a shell, I felt tumbled about, rolled, torn away from land.

I, Alisa Soto, was the daughter of a witch and a nonwitch. I was half witch. Half *witch*. Everything I had always thought about my mom my whole life had been a *lie*. A rough cry escaped my throat, and I quickly smothered it in a pillow. Everything I had known about *me* my whole life was a lie, too. It was *all* lies, and none of it made sense. Suddenly furious, I picked up the damn witch's box and threw it across my room as hard as I could. It smashed against one wall and shattered into dozens of sharp pieces. Just like my heart.

"Honey, are you all right?" My dad's voice sounded tentative, worried.

I'm fine, Dad. Except for the fact that you married a *witch* and now *I* have witch blood in me, just like all the people who *freak me out.*

"Can I come in?" Of course the door was locked, but it was one of those useless dinky locks where a little metal key pops it open in about a second. Dad, assuming his parental right, unlocked the door and came in.

I was curled up on my bed, under all my covers, with my grandmother's afghan bunched around my neck. I felt cold and miserable and hadn't gone down to dinner, which had been a chickpea casserole. As if I didn't feel bad enough.

My brain had been in chaos all afternoon. Dad must not have known Mom was a witch. I think she had hidden it from him—and who wouldn't—and he had never figured it out. He'd never been thrilled about my going to Kithic circles, but he hadn't acted paranoid. Surely he would have said something if he'd known my mom had been a witch.

"I brought you some soup," he said, looking for a place to put down the tray.

"Don't tell me. Tofu soup with organic vegetables who willingly gave their lives for the greater good." Spread the misery around.

He gave me a Look and set the tray at the bottom of the bed. "Campbell's chicken noodle," he said dryly. "I found some in the pantry. It's not even Healthy Request."

I sniffed warily. Real soup. Suddenly I was a little hungry. I sat up and dipped a saltine (okay, it was whole wheat) into the soup and ate it.

"What's wrong, honey?" Dad asked. "Do you feel like you're getting sick again? Like last month?"

I wish. This was so much worse. Then tears were rolling down my face and into my bowl.

"Nothing's wrong," I said convincingly. Sniff, sniff.

"Hilary says you seemed upset when she came home." Translation: You've been being a jerk again, haven't you?

I didn't know what to say. Part of me wanted to blurt out everything, show Dad the letters, confide in him. Another part of me didn't want to ruin whatever memories he had of my mom. And *another* part didn't want him to look at me, for the rest of my life, and think, "Witch," which he definitely would once he read the letters and understood about blood witches. My shoulders shook silently as I dipped another cracker and tried to eat it.

"Honey, if you can't tell me, maybe Hilary—I mean, if it's a girl thing . . ."

As if. My soggy cracker broke off in the soup and started to dissolve.

"Or me. You can tell me anything," he said awkwardly. I wished that either one of us thought that was true. "I mean, I'm just an old guy, but I know a lot."

"That's not true," I said without meaning to. "There's a lot you don't know." I started crying again, thinking about my mom, about how my whole childhood had been a lie.

"So tell me."

I just cried harder. There was no way I could possibly tell

him about this. It was like I had spent fifteen years being one person and suddenly found out I was someone completely different. My whole world was dissolving. "I can't. Just leave me alone, please."

He sat for a few more minutes but didn't come up with a plan that would suddenly make everything all right, make up for us not being close, for me not having a mom, for him marrying Hilary next month. After a while I felt his weight leave my bed, and then the door closed behind him. If only I *could* talk to him, I thought miserably. If only I could talk to *someone*. Anyone who would understand.

And then I thought of Morgan.

"Morgan?" I called on Wednesday morning. I had been lurking in the parking lot, waiting for her and Mary K. to arrive. Mary K. had popped out of the car, looking cute and fresh, the way she always did. I'd waited till she'd gone off to hang with our other friends; then Morgan had wearily swung herself out of her humongous white car and I called to her. I'd seen Morgan in the morning before and wasn't sure it was smart to talk to her this early. Besides her usual non-morning-person vibe, today she looked a little haggard, like she hadn't been sleeping.

She turned her head, and I stepped forward and waved. I saw the faint surprise in her eyes—she knew I tried to avoid her sometimes. As I got closer, I saw that she was drinking a small bottle of orange juice, trying to slug it down before the bell rang. Hilary would be glad that at least Morgan was paying attention to her blood sugar.

"Hey, Alisa," Morgan said. "Mary K. went thataway." She

pointed to the main building of Widow's Vale High, then glanced around us, as if to assure herself she was actually at school.

"Uh, okay. But actually I wanted to talk to *you*," I said quickly.

She slurped her drink.

"Are you okay?" I couldn't help asking.

She nodded and wiped her mouth on her jacket sleeve. "Yeah. I just—didn't get much sleep last night. Maybe I'm coming down with something." She gave another sideways glance, and I wondered if she was supposed to meet someone.

"Well, I have to tell you—I took your book on Monday." There. I'd gotten it out.

She gave me a blank look.

"Your green book. That you had Monday in your backpack. Well, I took it."

Morgan's brows creased: The rusty gears of her brain were slowly creaking to a start as the OJ flowed into her system. She gave a quick glance over her shoulder to her backpack—the scene of the crime—as if clues would still be there. "Oh, that green book? The Book of Shadows? You took it? Why?"

"Yes. I took it on Monday. And I read it. And I need to talk to you about it."

Suddenly she looked more alert. "Okay. Do you still have it?"

"Yeah. I want to keep it. It's—it's about a woman named Sarah Curtis, who lived in Gloucester, Massachusetts, in the seventies."

"Uh-huh." Go on, and feel free to start making sense, Alisa.

I gulped down some chilly air, hating what was about to come out. "Sarah Curtis, from that book, the witch, was my mother. I'm pretty sure." Like, positive.

Morgan blinked and shifted her weight. "Why do you think that?" she said finally.

"My mom's name was Sarah Curtis, and she lived in Gloucester, Massachusetts. There were things in the diary that reminded me of things about my mom and that my dad has told me about her. And then, after I had read it, I went to the jewelry box she left me and found a secret compartment underneath. I opened it, and there were letters inside from an uncle I didn't know about, and he talked about magick. In one of the letters he said congratulations about your new daughter, Alisa. In Texas. Which is where I was born." I took a deep breath. "Sarah Curtis was a Rowanwand witch."

Now I had her complete attention. Her eyebrows raised up in pointy arches, and she seemed to stare right into my brain. "But your dad isn't, is he?" I shook my head. "So you think you're half witch?"

"Yes," I said stiffly.

She shifted her weight and glanced around again. What was with her? "Half witch. You. Jeez, how do you feel about it? It's kind of a shock."

I gave a dry laugh. "Shock doesn't cover it. I'm so—worried. Really, really upset. I never knew any of this. I don't think my dad knew about it, either. But all of a sudden I'm something I didn't know, and I'm just . . . freaking. I don't want to be a witch."

Nodding, Morgan looked understanding. "I know what you mean. I went through that last November. All of a sudden I was someone else."

I knew that was when she'd found out she was adopted. "It's just that you—and Hunter—and the others, well, it scares me, some of the things you do. And now I find out I'm just like you—" Okay, this was not putting it well. But Morgan didn't look offended.

"And you wish you weren't, and you're worried, and you don't know what it means."

"Yes." A rush of relief washed over me—she did understand. Someone understood what I was going through.

The first bell rang then, and we both jumped as if poked with a cattle prod.

"I'll never get used to that sound," Morgan said, looking at the students filing into the buildings. "Listen, Alisa, I know how you feel. It wasn't easy for me to find out about my heritage, either. But talking to people about it can help. Why don't you come to the next Kithic circle on Saturday? Everyone misses you. And you could talk to Hunter or me afterward. We could be your support group."

I thought for a moment. "Yeah, okay. Maybe I will." I looked down at my backpack. "So I can keep the book?"

Morgan looked at me. "I think it's already yours."

5.
Morgan

><"Before the dark wave could be reproduced pretty much anywhere, the most we could have pulled off would be an epidemic, like the plague. And that's so hit-or-miss."
—Doris Grafton, New York, 1972><

Why am I doing this? I asked myself. I was sitting in Das Boot in front of Hunter's house, trying to work up the courage to just walk in. Yes, I wanted to have dinner with him; yes, I wanted to hear more about Rose MacEwan's BOS; yes, I didn't mind escaping Mary K.'s "Thursday Dinner Special": spinach pie. But I also couldn't help feeling reluctant at having to see Daniel Niall again.

I cast my senses out before I got out of the car—not that being *in* the car, even with the doors locked, was really any protection at all. Not against a witch as strong as Ciaran. I felt nothing, reminded myself dryly that this was not neces- sarily a guarantee, then hurried up the uneven front walk to Hunter's house.

He answered the door before I knocked.

"Hey," he said, and that one word, plus the way he looked at me, dark and intense, made my knees go wobbly.

"Hi. I brought these," I said, thrusting a paper-wrapped cone of flowers at him. I was too young to buy wine but hadn't wanted to show up empty handed, so I'd gone to the florist on Main Street and picked out a bunch of red cockscomb. They were so odd looking, so bloodred, I couldn't resist them.

"Cheers." He looked pleased, and leaned down to kiss me. "Are you all right? Has anything out of the ordinary . . . ?"

"No." I shook my head. "So far, so good. I just can't shake the feeling. . . ."

Hunter pulled me close and patted my back. "I know."

"He could be *anywhere*."

He nodded. "I do know, sweetie. But all we can do is be on our best guard. And know that if he does try anything, we'll battle him together."

"Together," I said softly.

Hunter smiled. "Well, take off your jacket and come sit down. Everything's almost ready."

Hunter's dad came in and looked at the table set for three. Hunter went into the kitchen, and I was left awkwardly standing there with a man who distrusted me and quite justifiably hated my father.

"Hi, Mr. Niall," I said, managing a smile.

He nodded, then turned and went into the kitchen, where I heard murmured voices. My stomach knotted up, and I wished I were at home, scarfing down spinach pie.

Five minutes later we were sitting at the small table, the

three of us, and I was working my way through Hunter's pot roast with enthusiasm. A plate of Hunter's really good cooking went a long way toward making me able to stand Mr. Niall.

"Oh, so much better than spinach pie," I said, pushing my fork through a potato. I smiled at Hunter. "And you can *cook*." In addition to being a fabulous kisser, a strong witch, and incredibly gorgeous.

Hunter grinned back at me. Mr. Niall didn't look up. He was starting to lose his pinched look, I saw when I glanced at him. The first time I'd met him, he looked like someone had forgotten him under a cupboard—all gray and dried up. After more than a week, he was beginning to look more alive.

"Da, why don't you tell Morgan some of what you've been thinking about with Rose's book?" Hunter suggested. "The part about the spell against a dark wave?"

Mr. Niall looked like he'd suddenly bitten a lemon.

"Oh, you don't have to," I said, feeling a defensive anger kindle inside me. I clamped down on it.

"No, I want him to," Hunter persisted.

"I'm not ready," Daniel said, looking at Hunter. "I've gotten some help from the book, but not enough to discuss it."

Hunter turned to me, and I saw a muscle in his jaw twitching. "Da has been reading Rose's BOS. In it there are sort of clues that he thinks he could use to craft a spell, something that could possibly dismantle a dark wave."

"Oh my *God*. Mr. Niall—that's incredible!" I said sincerely.

Daniel set his napkin by his plate. Without looking at me, he said tersely, "This is all premature, Giomanach. I'm not getting enough from the book to make it work. And I don't think Ciaran's daughter should be included in our discussion."

Well, there it was, out in the open. I felt like the town tramp sitting in at a revival meeting.

Hunter became very still, and I knew enough to think, Uh-oh. His hands rested on the table on either side of his plate, but every muscle in his body was tensed, like a leopard ready to strike. I saw Mr. Niall's eyes narrow slightly.

"Da," Hunter said very quietly, and I could tell from the tone of his voice that they'd had this conversation before, "Morgan is not in league with Ciaran. Ciaran has tried to *kill* her. She herself put a watch sigil on him for the council. Now he's on his way here, or is already here, to confront her about it. They are on opposite sides. She could be in mortal danger." There was a terrible stillness in his voice. I'd heard him sound that way only a few times before, and always in intensely horrible situations. Hearing it now sent shivers down my spine. Coming had been a mistake. As I was debating whether or not I was brave enough to just get up, grab my jacket, and walk out to my car with as much dignity as possible, Mr. Niall spoke.

"Can we afford to take the chance?" His voice was mild, unantagonistic: He was backing down.

"The chance you're taking is not the one you think," Hunter said, not breaking his gaze.

Silence.

Finally Mr. Niall looked down at his plate. His long fingers tapped gently against the table. Then he said, "A dark wave is in essence a rip in what divides this world from the netherworld. The spell to cast a dark wave has several parts. Or at least, this is my working hypothesis. First, the caster would have to protect herself, or himself, with various limitations.

Then he or she would have to proscribe the boundaries of the dark wave when it forms so that it doesn't cover the entire earth, for example."

Goddess. I hadn't realized that was possible.

"The actual rip, for lack of a better word, would be caused by another part of the spell, and it basically creates an artificial opening between the two worlds," Mr. Niall went on. "Then the spell calls on dark energy, spirits, entities from the netherworld to come into this world. They form the dark wave and as a cloud of negative energy destroy anything that is positive energy. Which describes most of the things on the face of the earth."

"Are these ghosts?" I asked.

Mr. Niall shook his head. "Not exactly. For the most part, they've never been alive and have no individual identity. They seem to have just enough consciousness to feel hunger. The more positive energy they absorb, the stronger they are the next time. The dark waves of today are infinitely stronger than the one Rose unleashed three hundred years ago. Then the last part of the spell gathers this energy in and sends it back through the rip."

I thought. "So an opposite spell would have to take into account all the parts of the original spell. And then either permanently seal the division between the two worlds or disband the dark energy."

"Yes," Mr. Niall said. He seemed to be loosening up slightly. "I think I can somehow do this—if I have enough time, and if I can decipher enough of Rose's spell. I have knowledge of the dark waves, and my wife was a Wyndenkell, a great spellcrafter. But it's starting to look as if Rose was careful not to put the information I need in writing."

It was my ancestor who started all this, I thought glumly. It runs in my family. My family. I looked up. "Could I see Rose's book again, please?"

Hunter immediately got up and left the room. Mr. Niall opened his mouth as if to object, then thought better of it. In moments Hunter was back with the centuries-old, disintegrating Book of Shadows. I opened it carefully, trying not to harm the brittle pages.

"Does either of you have an athame?" I asked. Wordlessly Hunter went and got his. "Hold it over the page," I told him. "See if anything shows up."

"I've tried this already," Mr. Niall huffed.

"Da, I think you underestimate the benefit of Morgan's unusual powers," Hunter said evenly. "Beyond that, she's a descendant of Rose. She may connect with her writing in ways that you and I can't."

Hunter slowly moved the flat of the knife blade over the page, and we all peered at it. When I had first found my mother, Maeve's, Book of Shadows, I had used this technique to illuminate some hidden writing. I had a feeling it might work again.

"I don't see anything." Hunter sighed.

I took the athame and slid the book closer to me. I let my mind sink into the page covered with tiny, spidery writing, its ink long faded to brown. Show me, I thought in a singsong. Show me your secrets. Then I slowly moved the athame over the page, just as Hunter had done. Show me, I whispered silently. Show me.

The sudden tension of both Hunter and Mr. Niall's bodies

alerted me to it even before my eyes picked up on it. Below me on the page, fine, glowy blue writing was shimmering under the knife blade. I tried to read it but couldn't—the words were strange, and some of the letters I didn't recognize.

Taking a deep breath, I straightened up and put the athame on the table. "Did you recognize those words?" I asked.

Mr. Niall nodded, looking into my face for the first time all evening. "They were an older form of Gaelic." Then he picked up the athame and held it over the page. For a long minute nothing happened; then the blue writing shone again. Mr. Niall's eyes seemed to drink it up. "This is it," he said, awe and excitement in his voice. "This is the kind of information I need. These are the secret clues I've been looking for." He looked at me with grudging respect. "Thank you."

"Nicely done, Morgan," said Hunter. I smiled at him self-consciously and saw pride and admiration in his eyes.

All of a sudden I felt physically ill, as if my body had been caught in a sneak attack by a flu virus. I realized I had a headache and felt achy and tired. I needed to go home.

"It's late," I said to Hunter. "I better get going."

Mr. Niall looked at me as I turned to go. "Cheers, Morgan."

"Bye, Mr. Niall." I looked at Hunter. "What about the writing? Will it disappear if I leave?"

Hunter shook his head. "You've revealed it, so it should be visible for at least a few hours. Long enough for Da to transcribe it." Hunter got my jacket and walked me out onto the porch. We both gave a quick glance around and felt each other cast our senses.

"Let me get my keys," he said. "I'll follow you to your house."

I shook my head. "Let's not go through this again." Hunter was always trying to protect me more than I was comfortable with.

"How about if I just sleep outside your house, then, in my car?"

I looked up at him with amusement and saw he was only half joking. "Oh, no," I protested. "No, I don't need you to do that."

"Maybe *I* need to do it."

"Thank you—I know you're worried about me. But I'll be okay. You stay here and help your dad decipher Rose's spell. I'll call you when I get home, okay?"

Hunter looked unsure, but I kissed him good night about eight times and got into my car. It wasn't that I felt I was invincible—it was just that when you go up against someone like Ciaran, there isn't a whole lot you can do except face it. I knew he wanted to talk to me; I also knew that he would, when he wanted to. Whether Hunter was there or not.

As I drove off, I saw Hunter standing in the street, watching me until I turned the corner.

I felt like crap by the time I pulled into my driveway. I got out of Das Boot and locked it, grimaced at its blue hood that I still hadn't gotten painted, and headed up the walk. The air didn't smell like spring, but it didn't smell like winter, either. My mom's dying crocuses surrounded me.

It wasn't really that late—a little after nine. Maybe I

would take some Tylenol and watch the tube for a while before I went to bed.

"Morgan."

My hand jerked away from the front door as if electrified. Every cell in my body went on red alert: my breathing quickened, my muscles tightened, and my stomach clenched, as if ready for war.

Slowly I turned to face Ciaran MacEwan. He was handsome, I thought, or if not strictly handsome, then charismatic. He was maybe six feet tall, shorter than Hunter. His dark brown hair was streaked with gray. When I looked into his eyes, brownish hazel and tilted slightly at the corners, it was like looking into my own. The last time I had seen him, he had taken the shape of a wolf, a powerful gray wolf. When the council had suddenly arrived, he had faded into the woods, looking back at me with those eyes.

"Yes?" I said, willing myself to appear outwardly calm.

He smiled, and I could understand how my mother had fallen in love with him more than twenty years ago. "You knew I was coming," he said in his lilting Scottish accent, softer, more beguiling than Hunter's crisp English one.

"Yes. What do you want?" I crossed my arms over my chest, trying not to show that inside, my mind was racing, wondering if I should send a witch message to Hunter, if I should try to do some sort of spell myself, if I could somehow just disappear in a puff of smoke. . . .

"I told you, Morgan. I want to talk to you. I wanted to tell you I forgive you for the watch sigil. I wanted to try once again to convince you to join me, to take your rightful place as the heir to my power."

"I can't join you, Ciaran," I said flatly.

"But you can," he said, stepping closer. "Of course you can. You can do anything you want. Your life can be whatever you decide you want it to be. You're powerful, Morgan—you have great, untapped potential. Only I can really show you how to use it. Only I can really understand you—because we're so much alike."

I've never been good at holding my temper, and more than once my mouth has gotten me into trouble. I continued that tradition now, refusing to admit to a fear close to terror. "Except one of us is an innocent high school student and the other of us is the leader of a bunch of murdering, evil witches."

For just a moment I saw a flash of anger in his eyes, and I quit breathing, both dreading what he would do to me and wishing it were already over. My knees began to tremble, and I prayed that they wouldn't give way.

"Morgan," he said, and underlying his smooth voice was a fine edge of anger. "You're being very provincial. Unsophisticated. Close-minded."

"I know what it means." He wouldn't even need to hear the quaver in my voice—he was able to pick up on the fact that my nerves were stretched unbearably taut.

"Then how can you bear to lower yourself to that level? How can you be so judgmental? Are you so all-seeing, all-knowing that you can decide what's right and wrong for me, for others? Do you have such a perfect understanding of the world that you assume the authority to pass judgment?

Morgan, magick is neither good nor evil. It just is. Power is neither good nor evil. It just is. Don't limit yourself this way. You're only seventeen: You have a whole life of making magick—beautiful, powerful magick—ahead of you. Why close all the doors now?"

"I may not be all-knowing, but I know what's right for me. I've figured out that it's wrong to wipe out whole villages, whole covens in one blow," I said, trying to keep my voice down so no one inside could hear me. "There's no way you can justify that."

Ciaran took a deep breath and clenched his fists several times. "You are my daughter; my blood is in your veins. I'm your family. I'm your father—your *real* father. Join with me and you'll have a family at last."

The quick pang of pain inside didn't distract me. "I have a family."

"They're not witches, Morgan," he said painstakingly, as if I were an idiot. "They can neither understand you nor respect your power—as I can. It's true, I'm selfish. I want the pleasure of teaching you what I know, of seeing you bloom like a rose, your extraordinary powers coming to fruition. I want to experience that with you. My other children—are not as promising."

I thought of my half brother Killian, the only one of Ciaran's other children I had met. I had liked Killian—he'd been fun, funny, irreverent, irresponsible. But not good material as an heir to an empire of power. Not as good as I would be.

"And you . . . you are the daughter of my mùirn beatha dàn," he said softly. His soul mate, my mother.

"Who you killed," I said just as softly, without anger. "You can ask me from now until I die, but I won't ever join you. I can't. In the circle of magick, I'm in the light. My power comes from the light, not the dark. I don't want the power of the dark. I will never want the power of the dark." I really hoped that was true.

"You will change your mind, you know," he said, but I detected a faint note of doubt in his voice.

"No. I can't. I don't want to."

"Morgan—please. Don't make me do this."

"Do what?" I asked, a thread of alarm lacing through me.

He sighed and looked down. "I was so hoping you'd change your mind," he said, almost to himself. "I'm sorry to hear that you won't. A power like yours—it must be allied with mine, or it presents too much of a risk."

"What the hell do you mean by that?"

He looked up at me again. "There's still time to change your mind," he said. "Time to save yourself, your family, your friends. If you make the right decision."

"You tell me what you're talking about," I demanded, my throat almost closed with fear. I thought of what he could to me, to the people I loved inside this house. To Hunter. "*Save* myself, my family? Don't you dare do *anything*. You asked your question. I answered. Now get away from me." I was almost shaking with rage and terror, remembering all too well the nightmare of New York, when he had tried to make me relinquish my power, my very soul to him. I remembered, too, the terrifying, heady sweetness of being a wolf alongside him, a ruthless, beautiful predator with indescribable strength. Oh, Goddess.

"I'll leave," Ciaran said, sounding sad. "I won't ask you again. It's a pity it all has to end this way."

"End *what* way?" I practically shrieked, almost hysterical.

"You've chosen your fate, daughter," he said, turning to leave. "It isn't what I wanted, but you leave me no choice. But know that by your decision you have sacrificed not only yourself, but everyone and everything you love." He gave a rueful, bitter smile. "Good-bye, Morgan. You were a shining star."

I felt ready to jump out of my skin and tried to choke out something, something to make him explain, make him tell me what he was going to do. Then I remembered: I knew his true name! The name of his very essence, the name by which I could control him absolutely. The name that was a color, a song, a rune all at once. Just as the name sprang to my trembling lips, Ciaran faded into the night. I blinked and peered into the darkness but saw nothing: no shadow, no footprints on the dead grass, no mark in the cold dew that was just starting to form.

Abruptly my knees finally gave way and I sat down, hard, on the cold cement steps. My breath felt cold and caught in my throat. My hands were shaking—I felt stupid with panic, with dread. As soon as I could get to my feet, I went inside, smiled, and said good night to my family. Then I went upstairs and called Hunter. And told him that Ciaran had gotten in touch with me.

The next morning Hunter was waiting for me outside my house when Mary K. and I came out to go to school.

"Hi, Hunter!" my sister said, looking surprised but pleased to see him at this hour.

"Hullo, Mary K.," he said. "Mind if I tag along this morning?"

Bewildered, my sister shrugged and got into the backseat of Das Boot. He and I exchanged meaningful glances.

For the rest of the day, Hunter hung out in my car outside school. Last night I had been inside my spelled house. Today, at school, I didn't have much protection. Whenever I passed a window, I looked out to see him. Even though he and I both knew this was like erecting a tissue-paper house in front of a gale-force wind, still, it made both of us feel better to be close.

At lunch he joined me and the members of Kithic in the cafeteria. After we'd talked last night, we'd agreed not to say anything to the rest of our coven until we knew more about what was going on.

"Hi, Hunter," said Bree, taking the seat next to him. "What are you doing here?"

"Just missed my girl, I guess," Hunter said, accepting half the sandwich I offered him. He immediately changed the subject. "So you're all coming to the next circle, right? At Thalia's?"

I saw Bree's beautiful, coffee-colored eyes narrow a fraction and thought it lucky that Thalia didn't go to our school. She had made it no secret that she found Robbie attractive. Privately I thought a bit of competition might be good for Bree—it was something she'd never had before.

Raven Meltzer clomped over in her motorcycle boots and sat down at the end of the table. She looked uncharacteristically sedate today, in a torn black sweatshirt, men's suit trousers, and less than half an inch of makeup. She nodded at the rest of the table, then surveyed her bought lunch without enthusiasm.

I looked around at my coven, my friends, remembering Ciaran's words from last night: He had said that with my decision, I had sacrificed them. At the start of the school year I had really known only Bree and Robbie. Now all of them—Jenna, Raven, Ethan, Sharon, and Matt—felt like an extended family. Despite how different we were, despite what other groups we belonged to, we were a coven. We had made magick together. And now, because of me, they might all be in serious danger. I took in a couple of shuddering breaths and opened my carton of chocolate milk. Hunter and I would somehow fix this situation. I had to believe that.

After school I joined Hunter at Das Boot. We gave Mary K. a ride home and picked up his car, and then we both drove to his house. Once there, he called upstairs to his dad. Mr. Niall soon came down and greeted me with what seemed like a fraction more warmth than usual. I felt slightly encouraged as the three of us sat around the worn wooden table in the kitchen.

"Last night Ciaran asked you to join him," Hunter said, jumping right in. I tried to ignore Mr. Niall's visible flinch.

"Yes," I said. "He's asked before. I've always said no. I said no again last night. But this felt more final. He said he was sorry to hear it—but that I could still save myself, my friends, and my family—if I made the right decision."

"He said specifically your friends, your family?" Hunter asked.

"Yes."

Hunter and Mr. Niall met eyes across the table. Mr. Niall stretched his hands out on the table and looked at them. Finally he said, "Yes, I think that sounds like a dark wave."

My mouth dropped open—somehow, despite his implications, I hadn't let myself believe Ciaran could have meant that. "So you really think Ciaran would send a dark wave *here,* to Widow's Vale? For me?"

"That's what it sounds like," said Mr. Niall, and Hunter nodded slowly. "Though it would likely be targeted to attack only the coven members and their families, and not the whole town."

"I agree with Da," said Hunter. "From what you told me last night, it sounds like Ciaran thinks your power is just too strong to not be allied with his. And I would guess he also wants revenge since you won't join him. Not to mention the added bonus of taking a Seeker out at the same time."

As much as I had tried to deny the real threat behind Ciaran's words, as soon as Hunter said "dark wave," I knew he was right. Still, it felt like a fresh, crushing blow, and I took small, shallow breaths, trying to keep calm.

"I think he's been planning it for a while," Mr. Niall went on. "I've been feeling the effects this past week. There's a feeling of deadness, of decay in the air. An oppression. At first I thought it was my mind playing tricks on me. But now I'm certain my instincts are right—there's a dark wave coming."

In a flash I remembered Mom's crocuses dying in a row

beside the front walk. I thought of how the lawn hadn't begun to green up, though it was time. I thought of how awful I'd been feeling physically. "What can we do? How can we stop it?" I asked, trying not to sound completely terrified. Inside me, my mind was screaming, *There's no way to stop it, there's never been a way.*

"I contacted the council," Hunter answered me. "They were no help at all, as usual. They're looking for Ciaran, and now that they know he's here, they'll surround Widow's Vale."

"For me it means I'll devote all my time and energy to crafting a spell that could combat a dark wave," said Hunter's father. "I've been able to decipher a lot of the hidden writing in Rose's book. I've started to sketch out the basic form of the spell, its shape. I wish I had more time, but I'll work as fast as I can."

The weight of this hung over my head like an iron safe. This was happening because of *me. I* had caused this to happen. Ciaran was my biological father—and because of that, everything I held dear would be destroyed. "What if I left town?" I suggested wildly. "If I left town, Ciaran would come after just me and leave everyone else alone."

"No!" Hunter and his father cried at the same time.

Taken back by their vehemence, I started to explain, but Mr. Niall cut me off.

"No," he said. "That doesn't work. I know that all too well. It won't really solve anything. It wouldn't guarantee the town's safety, and you'd be as good as dead. No, we have to face this thing head-on."

"What about the rest of Kithic?" I asked. "Shouldn't they know? Could they help somehow? All of us together?"

Looking uncomfortable, Hunter said, "I don't think we should tell Kithic."

"What? Why not? They're in danger!"

Hunter stood and put the kettle to boil on the stove. When he turned back, his face looked pained. "It's just—this is blood witch business. We're not supposed to involve non-witches in our affairs. Not only that, but there's truly nothing they can do. They might have strong wills, but they have very little power. And if we tell them, they probably wouldn't believe us, anyway. But if they did, then everyone would panic, which wouldn't help anything."

"So we just have to pretend we don't know everyone might die," I said, holding my head in my hands, my elbows on the table.

"Yes," Hunter said quietly, and once again I was reminded of the fact that he was a council Seeker and that he'd had to make hard decisions, tough calls, as part of his job. But I was new to it, and this hurt me. It was going to be literally painful not to tell my own family, or Bree, Robbie. . . . I swallowed hard.

"There's something else," Mr. Niall said. "I haven't mentioned this to you yet," he told Hunter. "With this type of spell, actually, as with most spells, the person who casts it will have to be a blood witch and will also have to be physically very close to where the dark wave would originate. My guess is that Ciaran would use the local power sink to help amplify the wave's power."

I nodded slowly. "That makes sense." At the edge of

town is an old Methodist cemetery where several magickal "leys" cross. That made that area a power sink: any magick made there was stronger. Any inherent blood witch powers were also stronger there.

"The problem, of course," Mr. Niall went on, "is that to be close enough to cast the spell, a witch is in effect sacrificing herself or himself because it will most likely cause death."

"Even if the spell works and the wave is averted?" I asked.

Hunter's dad nodded. The sudden whistle of the kettle distracted us, and Hunter mechanically made three mugs of tea. I gazed numbly at the steam rising from mine, then flicked my fingers over it widdershins and thought, Cool the fire. I took a sip. It was perfect.

"Well, that's a problem," Hunter said.

"No, it isn't," said Mr. Niall. "I'll cast the spell."

Hunter stared at him. "But you just said it would probably kill the caster!"

His father seemed calm: his mind had been made up for a while. "Yes. There are only so many blood witches around Widow's Vale. I'm the logical choice—I'm crafting the spell, so I'll know it best—and I would once again be with my mùirn beatha dàn."

Hunter had told me the loss of his mother, just a few months ago, had almost destroyed his father.

"I just got you back!" Hunter said, pushing away from the table. "You can't possibly do this! There has to be some other witch who would be a better choice."

Mr. Niall smiled wryly. "Like a witch with terminal cancer? All right, we can look for one." He shook his head.

"Look, lad, it's got to be me. You know it as well as I do."

"I'm stronger," Hunter said, wearing the determined look that I knew so well. "I should cast it. I'm sure I could survive. You could teach me the spell."

Mr. Niall shook his head.

"Dammit, I won't let you!" Hunter's loud voice filled the small kitchen. If he'd yelled at me like that, I would have been appalled, but his father seemed unmoved.

"It's not your decision, lad," he said. Calmly he picked up his mug of tea and drank.

"How long do we have?" I whispered, running my hands over the worn surface of the tabletop. "Is it tomorrow, or next week, or . . ."

Mr. Niall put down his mug. "It's impossible to say for certain." He looked at Hunter. "I would say, given the level of decay in the air and what I've read about the effects of an oncoming wave . . . perhaps a week. Perhaps a little less."

"Oh, *Goddess!*" I put my head down on the table and felt tears welling up behind my eyes. "A week! You're saying we might have one week left on this planet, a week before our families all die? All because of *me*? All because of my father?"

Mr. Niall surveyed me with an odd, grave expression. "I'm afraid so, lass." He stood. "I'm going back to work." Without a good-bye he left the room, and I heard him go upstairs.

"I just got him back," Hunter said, sounding near tears. I looked up from the table and realized, all at once, that no matter what happened to my family, Hunter was certainly going to lose his father. I stood up and wrapped my arms around him, pulling him close. So many times he had comforted me, and now I was glad to have the chance to give some back to him.

"I know," I said softly.

"He's got years left. Years to teach me. For me to get to know him again."

"I know." I held his head against my chest. His body was tight with tension.

"Bloody hell. This can't get any worse."

"It can always get worse," I said, and we both knew it was true.

6.
Alisa

>.<'It is the International Council of Witches'
considered opinion that the phenomenon of the
"dark wave of destruction" is without question the
most evil spell a witch can perpetrate. To create,
call on, participate in, or use such evil is the very
antithesis of what being a witch should be."

—Dinara Rafferty, ICOW Elder,
Loughrea, Ireland, 1994 >.<

"Can I get you anything? I'm running to the store." Hilary's
voice interrupted my reading, and I glanced up as the door
to my room opened. There she was, in black leggings and a
red tunic, her artificially streaked hair held back by a red
Alice band.

"No. I'm okay," I said, raising my voice so she could hear
me over my CD player.

"Ginger ale? That's what I like when I'm sick."

"No thanks."

I won the stare-down contest and when Hilary finally
broke, I went back to my reading. A minute later I heard the
front door close with a little more force than necessary. I
had elected to take a mental health day—going to school,

having PE, eating lunch with people, paying attention in class—it all seemed ridiculous compared to finding out I was half witch. Thus my "illness" that Hilary was trying to treat. But she was gone now, and I had peace and quiet.

I pulled Sarah Curtis's Book of Shadows from under my bed and then got the small pile of letters. Since Tuesday, I had read all of them. It was like trying to absorb the news that a huge meteor was hurtling toward Earth—on some level, I just couldn't comprehend it. I mean, until a month or two ago I hadn't even known that real blood witches existed, and I kind of hadn't even believed it until I had seen Morgan Rowlands and Hunter Niall do things that couldn't be explained any other way. And now, surprise! I was half of something weird myself. Not only that, but my mom had pretty much felt the same way about being a witch—it had scared her, too, and before she met my dad, she had actually stripped herself of her powers. Which would explain why he didn't know she was a witch.

I had a lot to take in—my mother being a witch, her stripping herself of her powers, which I didn't even know you could do, and also about her family. Dad had always said that Mom had a falling-out with her family before he met her. He'd never known any of them. From the Book of Shadows and Sam Curtis's letters, it was starting to look more like they had disinherited her when she stripped herself of her powers. So unless they had all been wiped out by a freak accident after my mother left Gloucester, there might actually still be some relatives living there. I guessed it was *possible* they were all dead—GLOUCESTER FAMILY DECIMATED BY ROGUE TORNADO—but that seemed kind of unlikely.

Mom had been a Rowanwand. I knew from what Hunter

had said in circles that Rowanwands in general had a reputation for being the "good guy" witches. They were dedicated to knowledge, they helped other witches, they had all sworn to do no evil, to not take part in clan wars. That didn't fit me at all. Dedicated to knowledge? I hated school. Sworn to do no evil? It seemed like every ten minutes, I was harshing out on someone. So I didn't feel very Rowanwandish. Which was a good thing, in my opinion.

Maybe being a witch was like a recessive gene, and you had to have copies from both parents in order for it to kick in. That would be cool. I breathed out, already feeling relieved. Since Dad was normal, maybe I only *carried* the witch gene, but it wouldn't be expressed. I frowned, thinking back to last semester's biology class. Pea plants and fruit flies popped into my mind, but what about recessive witch genes? Or was it even a gene? But what else could it be?

I groaned and leaned back against my pillows. Now I really did have a headache. I went to the bathroom and took some Tylenol and was just climbing back into bed when I heard the front door shut again downstairs. Feeling my nerves literally fraying, I pushed the letters and book under my covers and picked up *The Crucible,* which we were studying in sophomore English, ironically enough.

I was just making a mental note to pick up the Cliffs Notes for it when lo and behold, Hilary popped her head around my door because I had *forgotten to lock it.* She was carrying a tray that had a sprout-filled sandwich on it and some teen magazines that had articles like "Are You Over Your Ex? Take This Quiz and Find Out!"

For those of us who are too dumb to figure it out ourselves.

"Alisa? I thought you might be hungry. When I was sick, my mom always brought me lunch and some fun magazines."

"Oh. Thanks," I said unenthusiastically. At the risk of stating the obvious, you're not my mom. "I think I really just want to be left alone, though."

Her face fell, and I immediately felt a pang of guilt.

"I know I'm not your mom," she said, obvious hurt in her voice. "But would it be so hard for us to be friends? In a little while we're going to be related. I mean, like it or not, Alisa, your dad and I are getting married, and this baby I'm having is your half brother or half sister."

She set the tray down on my bed, and at that moment my CD player popped loudly. I smelled an electric burning smell and jumped up to unplug it. It was practically brand-new! Why did everything keep self-destructing around me? Hilary gave me a long-suffering look, then swirled out of the room, slamming the door behind her.

I looked down at the plug in my hand, beginning to feel like a walking destructive force: just a few days ago, the butter dish at Mary K.'s, then my jewelry box, now the CD player. . . .

Oh my God. My breath froze in my throat. I stood stock-still, petrified by a sudden thought. I had just read about this kind of stuff in my mom's journal. When she'd been younger, she'd caused weird telekinetic things to happen—things fell off shelves, radios quit working, car horns wouldn't stop honking. Watches never worked on her—or on me, either. The batteries died instantly.

I breathed very shallowly. The horrible, unavoidable realization coming over me felt like a wave of icy water. I went through all the weird things that had happened around me for the last couple of months. Things breaking. Things falling off shelves. Things that had stopped working. I had been so sure that stuff had been caused by Morgan, with her scary powers.

The lightbulbs popping at our circle. The bookcase falling at the library. And sometimes they had happened without Morgan being there. Like on Tuesday—the jewelry box. I felt like I had been blind and now could suddenly see everything.

Crash! Pop!

I spun around to see my little collection of crystal animals fall off their shelf, one by one, and shatter on the floor. *Stop!* I thought desperately, and a small unicorn teetered on the edge of the shelf but didn't fall.

Oh God, oh God, oh God. Numbly I stared down at the shattered animals, then up at the rest of the collection. The shelf looked rock solid. Unless a tiny, unnoticeable earthquake had just shaken Widow's Vale, I had some awful truths to face.

It had been *me*. I had caused that to happen. I had caused the CD player to self-destruct. I had caused my jewelry box to leap off my dresser. Why hadn't that struck me as more odd? I mean, how good was I at lying to myself? All this time I had blamed Morgan and avoided her for being freaky and hated the things that I thought her powers did.

But it had been *me*, with my mom's witch gene, all along. Just like my mom, I was a walking telekinetic nightmare. God, my mother had been a full blood witch, and she couldn't even control her own powers. What was going to happen to *me*?

Thalia Cutter lived on Montpelier Avenue. Dad gave me a ride over on Saturday night. I hadn't mentioned that it was a circle, and he hadn't asked. It had taken me all day to psych myself into going. But in the end I accepted that this was probably the only place I could find help or information.

"Thanks, Dad," I said, opening my door.

"Call me when you need me to come get you," he said.

"Okay. Or maybe I can get a ride."

"Alisa—" He leaned out toward me, but stopped as if he'd changed his mind. "Have a good time."

"Thanks." I left him and headed up the walk to the front porch, where I rang the bell.

"Alisa! Come on in," said Jenna, who opened the door.

"Hi." I've always liked Jenna—she's really nice.

Other people greeted me: Ethan Sharp, who had been one of the biggest potheads in school; Simon Bakehouse and Raven Meltzer, who had both been in the original Kithic with me. Raven cracks me up. I was dumping my jacket on a sofa when I felt a prickling at the base of my neck. Turning around, I saw that Hunter Niall and Morgan were coming in together.

It was a fact: Hunter was *hot,* even though he was four years older than me, a witch, and went out with Morgan. Despite all those drawbacks, he tended to cause a lot of head turning when he walked into a room. And even though right then he looked like he was hung over and simultaneously fighting a virus, I felt a little quiver when he saw me and immediately came to talk to me.

"Hey, Hunter," I said.

"Hi," he said, bending down to talk to me. I'm not a shrimp, but he's over six feet tall. "Morgan told me about what you just found out." He stopped and gave a grin that would have melted Alaska. He's usually kind of serious, so when he does smile, everyone's knees go weak. Or at least I'm assuming I'm not the only one. "I would say congratulations, but I understand you don't feel that way."

My cheeks burned, and I looked away. "No."

He immediately sobered and leaned closer so only I could hear. "I know it must have been a shock. And I understand how you've been feeling about magick and witches. I'd like to talk to you about it, try to help if I can."

I nodded. "Thanks." I stood very still, waiting for a picture to fall off the wall, the door to fly open, or a window to crack. Nothing happened, and I held my breath, determined to stay very, very calm this evening.

Hunter went back to Morgan's side, and I saw that she looked pretty bad, too. They must have been passing germs back and forth. Yuck.

"We can get started," said Hunter. "I think everyone's here. Is there any coven business first? I think Simon has volunteered to host next Saturday, right? Good. Okay, now. Tonight I'd like to talk a bit about magick."

Hunter knelt and drew a large circle on Thalia's living-room floor. He always started by drawing a circle, but this time he added another circle around it and then one more circle around that. Then he took a small cloth bag of stones and placed different-colored stones around the outside circle. Standing, he gestured us into the little "door" he had left, and once we were all in the smallest circle, he closed the circles with chalk, stones, and also some runes that he traced in the air. I wondered what was going on.

"Now, magick," he said, rubbing the chalk off his hands. He looked pale and tired. "Magick is basically energy, life force, chi, whatever you want to call it. The same magick that makes a flower bloom, produces fruit on a tree, brings a baby into the world is the exact same magick that can light fires spontaneously, move objects, and work invisibly within the universal construct in order to effect change—such as casting a protective spell, a fertility spell, or a healing spell. Now, can I have each of your impressions about magick?"

He nodded to Sharon Goodfine.

She frowned thoughtfully, her shiny dark hair brushing her shoulders. "To me, magick is potential—the possibility of doing something."

"That's a nice thought," said Hunter. "Thalia?"

"It's just cool," she said, shrugging. "It's different, out of the ordinary."

Ethan said, "It's like a different kind of control, a different way of getting a handle on things."

"It's being connected with the life force," said Jenna.

"It's beautiful," Bree said.

Next was Morgan. "It's . . . another dimension to life, an added meaning to regular life. It's a power and a responsibility."

Hunter nodded again. "Robbie?"

"It's mysterious," said Robbie.

"Alisa, how about you?" Hunter asked.

"It's scary," I said abruptly, thinking of my own experiences with it. As soon as I said that, all my feelings came rushing out. "It's uncontrollable. It's dangerous. It's awful, like having some genetic error. You never know when it's going to wreck your life."

My fists were clenching, and my mouth felt tight. I realized I was surrounded by silence and looked up to see eleven pairs of eyes watching me. Nine pairs were surprised. Hunter was calm, accepting. Morgan looked understanding.

"Oh. Did I say that out loud?" I said, feeling embarrassed.

"It's all right," Hunter said. "Magick strikes everyone differently. I understand how you feel." He turned to the others. "Now, since we have stones of protection, I won't call on earth, air, fire, or water. But I do cast this circle in the name of the Goddess and the God and ask them to join us and bless our power tonight. Join hands."

I took hold of Simon's hand and Raven's, feeling an impending sense of doom. If I was in this circle and it got all magicky, what would happen? What would I destroy?

Slowly we began to walk deasil, clockwise. Hunter started a chanting kind of song. It was incredibly pretty and easy to follow, and soon all of us were joining in. It was kind of like aural Prozac, because soon I began to feel calmer and more cheerful than I had in days. I felt like everyone here was my friend, that I was safe, that we were singing the most beautiful song, that I was filled with a light that made all my troubles seem bearable.

I was processing these feelings, and suddenly I realized that this was magick, too. This was a positive, gentle kind of magick. As the chant rose and grew, I felt better and better. It was like I was trying to worry about it being magick but just couldn't. I knew it was weird, but it all felt okay. When we threw our hands apart and raised our arms to the sky, I was smiling widely, feeling loose and open instead of tight and upset.

Our circle broke apart then, and people were hugging and patting each other's backs. Morgan came over to me and took my hand. She put her own palm on top of mine and held it there for a moment. She looked at her hand, and I felt a gentle heat. I took my hand away, and there was a rose-colored rune imprinted on my skin.

I grabbed her hand and looked at her palm. Nothing was there. I rubbed at my hand and realized that the rune was *raised,* it was my *skin,* raised up, like a scar. I stared at it, and Morgan gave a little smile. "That's wynn," she said. "Happiness. Peace." She caught my expression and added, "It'll go away in a little while. It's just something to take away from here."

She went back to join Hunter, and I looked at my hand again. This was visible magick, right here on me. Peace, happiness. Did she just mean the rune or the actual feelings, too?

7.
Morgan

><"The first time I saw one was in Scotland. I didn't take part, of course—I wasn't strong enough yet. But I watched from a distance as it rolled across the countryside, purging the land of everything unclean. I almost wept with the glory of it."

—Molly Shears, Ireland, 1996><

On Sunday, I went to church with my family, despite feeling definitely ill. Afterward we went to the Widow's Diner, where I could only manage to choke down a few bites of my BLT.

At home I tossed down some sinus/allergy stuff, then changed, grabbed my keys, and yelled that I was going to Hunter's. When Sky had gone to France and then England, my parents had known that left Hunter with the house to himself. For a while they had given me squirrel eyes whenever I went there and again when I got back. Now that his father lived there, they were less suspicious. Of course, they hadn't met Mr. Niall and had no clue as to how different he was from their vision of a father.

Fatherly or not, his presence was enough to make me feel

weird about being alone with Hunter anywhere in his house. I sighed and got into Das Boot. Outside it was horrible— after a few misleading days of decent springlike weather, we had taken a big step backward, and it was in the midthirties, overcast, and smelling like snow. Before I reached Hunter's, tiny, icy raindrops starting pinging against my windshield.

"Hullo, my love," said Hunter as I approached the front door. He gave me a critical glance, then said, "How about some hot tea?"

"Do you have any cider?" I asked. "With spices in it? Or lemon?"

He nodded and I went in, glad to see the fireplace in the living room had been lit. I dropped my coat and stood before the fire, holding out my hands. The dancing flames were soothing. On his way to the kitchen, Hunter stopped in back of me, wrapped his arms around my chest, and held me close. I leaned back and let my eyes drift shut, feeling his warmth, the strength in his arms. One of his hands came up to stroke my hair, melting the few bits of ice crystal that lingered there. He leaned down and kissed my neck. I tilted my head to give him better access. Slowly he put careful kisses up my neck and across my jaw. I turned to face him and smiled wryly—he looked as bad as I felt. It seemed kind of pathetic, how bad we were both feeling, yet we still had such a strong desire to be in each other's embrace. His lips were very soft on mine, moving gently, afraid to make either of us feel worse.

When I heard Mr. Niall's footsteps on the stairs, Hunter and I untangled and headed toward the kitchen. Moments later Mr. Niall joined us, and Hunter started mulling cider on the stove. I sat glumly at the table, my pounding head resting in my hands.

"Why do we all feel so bad?" I asked. Mr. Niall looked pale and drawn.

"It's the effect of an oncoming dark wave," Hunter's father said with little energy. "It isn't even in force yet, but the spells to call it have been started and the place and people targeted. It isn't going to be long now. A matter of days."

"Oh, Goddess," I muttered, a fresh alarm racing through my veins.

"We'll feel sicker and sicker as the dark wave draws closer, and we'll grow irritable. Which is unfortunate, because we'll need to work with each other now more than ever."

Hunter sighed. "You talked to Alyce this morning?" he asked his father, and Mr. Niall nodded.

"She and the other members of Starlocket have been holding power circles, aiming their energy at Widow's Vale and at Kithic in particular. They're hoping to help in any way they can, but there's been so little documented evidence about anyone even trying to resist a dark wave." He ran his long-fingered, bony hand over his face.

"Have you had any progress?" I asked.

He let out a breath heavily, and his shoulders sagged. "I've been working day and night. In some ways I'm making progress. I'm crafting the form of the spell, its order, its words. But it would be much stronger if I could give it more specificity. If only I had more time."

I looked up and caught Hunter's eye. I knew we were feeling the same desperation, the same frustration: If only we could help Mr. Niall or speed him along. But we were helpless; we just had to hope that his father was up to the task.

"What do you mean by specificity?" I asked as Hunter

put a mug of cider in front of me, and I inhaled. The spices of ginger and cinnamon rose up to meet me. I drank, feeling its warmth soothing my stomach.

"The spell is basic," Mr. Niall said, sounding frustrated. "It's designed to cover a certain area, at a certain time, in a certain way. It's designed to combat a dark wave, to dismantle it. But it would be so much more powerful if I could use something particular against its creator."

"What would that do?" I needed a cold cloth for my forehead.

"Spells are just as personal as the way someone looks, like their fingerprints," Hunter explained. "If you're trying to dismantle or repel another witch's spell, your own spell greatly increases in power if you can imbue it with something in particular that identifies the spellcrafter you're working against. That's why in spells, you so often need a strand of hair or an item of clothing of the person who's the focus of the spell. It gives the spell a specific target."

"Like using an arrow instead of a club," said Mr. Niall.

I sat for a few moments, thinking. I had no strand of Ciaran's hair, none of his clothes. My head felt fragile, made of china that had been broken and poorly mended. It was a struggle to put two thoughts together.

Wait—I rubbed at my eyes, catching the elusive thought. I had . . . I had something of Ciaran's. I didn't even think of it as his anymore—it was completely mine now. But it had once been his. He had handled it. I drained my mug and stood up, feeling my muscles ache naggingly.

"I'll be back," I said, and left before either Hunter or Mr. Niall could open his mouth.

*   *   *

It was still raining sullenly as I climbed behind the wheel of my car. Inside, the vinyl seats were freezing, and I immediately cranked the heater. I pulled away from Hunter's curb and headed toward the road that would take me out of town.

Widow's Vale was surrounded by what had once been prosperous farmland and was now only a few small family holdings, bordered on all sides by abandoned fields, overgrown orchards, and woods of tall, second-growth trees.

There was a place along here, a patch of woods completely unmarked by any physical sign but still a place I recognized at once, as if there were a large arrow spray painted on a line of tree trunks. There it was. I pulled well over onto the road's shoulder, feeling the slipperiness of the ice-crusted gravel at the road's edge. Reluctantly I climbed out of my car, leaving its cozy warmth for the inhospitable sting of icy rain.

I pulled my collar up as far as I could and headed straight across a rough-cut field of withered grass stalks. At the first break in the woods I paused for a moment, then headed straight between two beech trees. This place was mine alone. I could feel the presence of no other human, witch or nonwitch. I felt safe here, safer than in town.

In the woods there was no path, no marked trail, but I slogged steadily forward, unerringly headed for the place that bore my spell and contained my secret. It was a good ten-minute walk—my clogs slid on the wet, decaying leaves, and tiny branches, still unbudded, whipped across my face and caught at my hair.

Then, in a small clearing, I lifted my face to the patch of bare, leaden sky. It was here, it was still here, and though animals had crisscrossed this place with any number of trails, no human had been here since my last time. Pausing, I closed my eyes and cast my senses out strongly, taking my time, going slowly, feeling the startled heartbeat of small animals, wet birds, and farther out, the still, wary eye of an occasional deer. At last I was quite sure I was still alone, and I walked out into the clearing and knelt on the sodden forest litter.

I'd brought no shovel with me, but Das Boot had a jack and a crowbar, and it was the crowbar I used, chucking it into the cold ground and twisting it. It didn't take long. I felt layer upon layer of my amateurish spells of protection, the best I had been able to do at the time. Then, feeling close, I used my fingers to claw at the freezing earth. Another two inches and my fingers scrabbled at wet cloth. I cleared the dirt away around it and soon lifted up a silken bundle. I didn't untie the knot that held the scarf's contents in place. I didn't need to. Instead I kicked the dirt back in place and lightly scattered some leaves and pine needles and twigs over the area until it again looked untouched. Picking up my crowbar, holding my cold, damp bundle, I headed back to my car.

"Where did you go?" Hunter asked when I returned. "Where have you been? I was worried sick! Don't go anywhere like that without telling me, all right?"

"I'm sorry." I was still chilled, my fingernails dirt-packed and broken. It seemed too hard to explain when my errand had taken so much effort. Instead I walked into Hunter's circle room, where Mr. Niall was kneeling on the floor, his eyes closed, surrounded by papers and books and candles. He felt me come in and looked up.

I knelt beside him, the knees of my jeans soaked. "Here," I

said, pulling the silk-wrapped package from my coat pocket. My fingers were cold and stiff as I picked at the knot, but I finally pulled it loose and the cloth fell open. I reached in to pick up the only thing of Ciaran's I had: a beautiful gold pocket watch, engraved with his initials and my mother's. Not only that—it had my mother's, Maeve's, image spelled into it. To be able to see my mother's face was a gift. To me it was a concrete reminder of the relationship my blood parents had once had—the only thing that was part of both of them. My mother was dead—the spell against Ciaran couldn't rebound on her. But Ciaran's vibrations ran all through it.

When Mr. Niall reached for it, I surprised myself by pulling my hand back. Embarrassed, I pushed the watch forward again. He could use it more than I. Maybe it was better not to have any reminders of a love that had ended so tragically—even though that same love had resulted in my birth. It suddenly struck me that my parents' relationship was the epitome of magick itself: darkness and light. A great, great love and a great, great hatred. Passion, both good and bad. A powerful joining followed by an irrevocable tearing apart. The rose and the thorn.

"This was Ciaran's," I explained, offering it to Mr. Niall. I forced my hand to stay open while he took it.

"When did you get it back?" Hunter asked, surprised.

"The last time Ciaran was here," I explained, feeling very tired.

"And you kept it?" Hunter knew as well as I how dangerous it could be to have something of someone who wants to control you.

"Yes. It was my mother's." I was aware I sounded defensive—I had kept this a secret, even from Hunter. "I buried it outside of town. I was going to leave it there until it had been purified, all its dark energy gone. Years."

Mr. Niall was examining the watch, turning it over in his hands. "I can use this," he said, as if talking to himself. He looked up. "But are you sure? It will be completely destroyed, you know."

I nodded, looking at the watch. "I know. It's okay. I don't need it anymore." Still, even as I said the words, something in me knew I'd feel its loss. I shivered from leftover chill.

When I looked up, Mr. Niall was watching me. "This will help," he said. "Thank you." His eyes looked at me as if he were seeing me for the first time. I got the impression I had just moved up several notches in his estimation.

"Okay, well, I'll get out of your way," I said, standing up. In the kitchen I washed my hands, soaping them over and over, holding them under the warm water as if I were washing off more than dirt. Then I went into the living room and sank down on the floor in front of the fireplace. Hunter sat down next to me, and soon I was warm enough to take off my coat. We scooted back until we could lean against the couch, and I rested my head against his shoulder. Gently Hunter lifted me up onto his lap so I was sitting sideways across his legs. With his arms around me, I felt incredibly safe and warm. I was so happy to be there that I didn't even care if Mr. Niall came out and found us like this.

"Thank you for making that sacrifice," Hunter murmured close to my ear. "Why didn't you tell me about it?"

I shrugged, not really knowing myself. "I knew I wasn't going to use it, not for a long time."

He nodded and kissed my ear. "I know what it must mean to you."

"Not as much as my life, your life, my family. My friends," I said, closing my eyes and snuggling closer.

"Morgan," he said, his voice low. I felt his fingers under my chin, raising my face so he could kiss me. It felt so good, so right, and it made everything else fade away: all my worries, the way I felt physically, the sadness of losing my watch. Ever since Hunter had gotten back from Canada, we hadn't had much time alone together. I'd been concerned about what I had seen— Hunter and the Canadian witch—and sometimes it made me feel insecure and out of sync with him. But right now those feelings were melting away, and once again I felt that quickening, that rush of desire that made me tremble.

We clung together, kissing, and I now knew him well enough for there to be comforting familiarity mixed in with the rush. I remembered the last night we'd been together, before he'd left for Canada. I had planned for us to make love for the first time: I'd actually started taking the Pill because I didn't know how witch birth control worked, I'd psyched myself up, shaved my legs, everything. And we had almost done it. We'd come so, so close. Then Hunter had talked me into waiting until after he got back from Canada so we wouldn't have to say good-bye afterward. Of course, we didn't know that he'd be bringing his dad back with him and that almost immediately we'd be threatened by a dark wave.

I gripped Hunter's collar in one hand and pulled him closer, kissing his mouth hard, feeling his fingers tighten around my waist. Hunter, I thought. I want to be joined with you. Are we ever going to get there? Or are we going to die before we get the chance?

8.
Alisa

><"Tonight we opened a rift in the world, in time, in life. I fell to my knees in awe as the source of our power swelled above my head. I could only stare in wonder as my coven leader called upon the dark power, right in front of us. Every day I thank the Goddess I found this coven, Amyranth."
— Melissa Felton, California, 1996><

"Alisa, are you okay?"

My head snapped up to see Mary K.'s big brown eyes gazing at me with concern. We were sprawled in Mary K.'s room after school on Monday, listening to music and sort of doing homework.

"I'm okay." I shook my head. "It's just, like, everything's coming down on me at once. It's giving me a headache."

Mary K. nodded sympathetically. "Everyone has a headache lately. It must be the weather." I was so glad that we were friends. My best friend had moved away at the end of last summer, and though I still missed her, being friends with Mary K. had helped a lot.

"Like the wedding and Ms. Herbert's science fair project?" she asked.

"Yeah." Oh, and the fact that I was half witch. That, too. I hadn't told Mary K. about my realization—I knew that she still had a problem with Morgan's involvement with Wicca, and I wasn't ready to test her reaction.

"Any ideas for the science project?"

I thought. "Maybe a life-size modeling-clay version of a digestive system?"

Mary K. giggled. "Fun. I'm thinking about something with plants."

"Can you be more specific?"

Her shiny russet hair bounced as she shook her head. "I haven't worked out the details."

We both laughed, and I pulled over the box of Girl Scout cookies and had another Thin Mint.

"Any wedding news?"

My eyes closed in painful memory. "Right now the flower-girl dress of choice is emerald green, which will basically make me look like I died of jaundice, and it has a big wide bow across the ass. Like, look at my humongous big butt, everyone! In case you missed it!"

"I still can't get over the fact that you're the *flower girl*," Mary K. laughed, falling back on her bed, and it was hard for me to remain sour.

"My backup plan is to break my leg the morning of the ceremony," I told her. "So I'll be bringing you a baseball bat soon, just in case."

I turned my attention back to my algebra problems. Art class I was good at. But all these little numbers jumping around the page just left me cold. "What did you get for the equation for number seven?" I asked, tapping my pencil against my teeth.

"A big blank. Maybe we should get Morgan."

"I'll get her," I said casually, getting to my feet. There was the slightest surprise in Mary K.'s eyes that I would voluntarily talk to the witch queen. "Where is she?"

"In her room, I think."

Mary K. and Morgan's rooms were connected by the bathroom they shared. The door to Morgan's room was ajar, and I tapped on it.

"Morgan?"

"Mpfh?" I heard in response, and I pushed open the door. Morgan was lying on her bed, a wet washcloth draped over her forehead. Her long hair spilled over the side of her bed. She looked awful.

As I approached the bed, she mumbled, "Alisa? What's up?" She hadn't opened her eyes, and I got a little nervous shiver from this evidence of her witch skills.

"How do you do that?" I asked quietly. "You can just feel someone's vibes or something? Or like my aura?"

At this Morgan did open her eyes and bunched her pillow under her head so she could see me. "I gave you a ride after school, so I knew you were here. I heard someone open the door and walk into my room. I knew it wasn't *me*. Mary K. sort of flounces through and makes more noise. That left you."

"Oh," I said, my cheeks flushing.

"Sometimes a cigar is just a cigar," she said.

I had no idea what that meant. "Anyway, Mary K. and I are stuck on an algebra problem. Could you come help us? If you're up to it, I mean." She looked really sick. "Do you have the flu or something? Why were you in school?"

Morgan shook her head and sat up very slowly, like an old lady. "No. I'm okay."

"Hunter's sick, too. Why didn't you just stay home?"

"I'm okay," she said, obviously lying. "How do *you* feel?"

"Uh, I have a little headache. Mary K. thinks it's the weather."

Our eyes met just then, and I swear Morgan looked like she wanted to say something, was about to say something.

"What?" I asked.

Standing up, Morgan pulled down her sweatshirt and flipped her hair over her shoulder. "Nothing," she said, heading toward the door. "What's this problem you need help with?"

There was more here than she was telling me. I knew it. Without thinking, I reached out to grab her sleeve, and at that exact instant there was a *thud* and a sound like glass hitting something. I looked around wildly, wondering what I had destroyed this time, feeling cursed.

"That was Dagda," Morgan explained, a tinge of amusement in her voice.

Sure enough, I now saw her small gray cat getting to his feet on the floor by Morgan's bed. He looked sleepy and irritated.

"Sometimes he rolls off the bed when he's asleep," Morgan said.

Frustrated, I pulled back my hand and curled and uncurled my fingers. There was something happening here, something I didn't know about. Something Morgan wasn't telling me. I remembered the other day, when Morgan had run out of the kitchen to talk to Hunter, how upset she had seemed. But her face was now closed, like a shade being pulled down, and I knew she wouldn't tell me. We went into Mary K.'s room, back to algebra and away from magick.

*   *   *

That night I was slumped on my bed, taking a magazine quiz to find out if I was a flirting master or a flirting disaster. By question five, things were looking bad for me. I tossed the magazine aside, my mind going back to Morgan. For some reason I had a terrible feeling—I couldn't even describe it. But I was somehow convinced that something weird or bad was happening, and that Morgan and Hunter knew about it, and that they were keeping it to themselves. But what could it be? They both looked physically ill. Morgan had seemed so close to saying something, something hard. And last week there had been a day when Hunter had sat outside school literally all day. I didn't think it was just because he couldn't stand to be away from her.

Sitting up, I decided to confront Morgan again. I would somehow make her tell me what was going on, what was wrong with her and Hunter. The flaws in this plan were immediately obvious: (1) I had already asked Morgan, and she'd made it clear that she wasn't going to tell me. (2) Mary K. would wonder why I needed to talk to Morgan. And if it *was* some weird witch thing, I didn't want to drag her into it.

So how could I find out?

Hunter.

No. I knew him, but we weren't good friends. I was kind of impressed by and wary of him at the same time. What would he think if I asked him to tell me their secret? Would he get mad at me?

Hunter was out. But—there really wasn't anyone else. I went through the members of Kithic in my mind. No one else had seemed nervous or ill. Just Morgan and Hunter. The blood witches. I shook my head. My brain kept coming back to this again and again, the way it had about my mother's green book. This felt the same.

I had to talk to Hunter.

I didn't have his phone number, but I knew where he lived. Now, did I have the nerve to ask him? I had no choice. I ran downstairs: Girl of Action. In the living room I encountered Hilary, watching a videotape of *Sex and the City*. Too late I remembered that Dad had gone to a union meeting at the post office, where he worked. Damn, damn, damn. I met Hilary's inquiring look. I had to go ahead and ask her.

"Um, I forgot my algebra book at school," I said, giving an Oscar-caliber performance. Not. "My friend has the same book and says I can borrow his. Do you think you could give me a ride to his house?"

Hilary actually looked touched to be asked, and I felt a little pang of guilt over the way I usually treated her. The fact that I would now owe her was not lost on me. Once again I wished the state of New York would lower the freaking driving age to, say, fifteen. Then I wouldn't have to ask anyone for favors.

"Sure," Hilary said easily. She clicked off the TV and stood up, stretching. She gave me a smile and almost looked pretty for a split second. "Let me go to the bathroom real quick. Since I've been pregnant, I have to pee every five minutes."

She turned and left the room then, so she didn't see the horrified expression on my face. Oh, gross! Why did I have to know *that*?

Not being a complete idiot, I held my tongue, and a few minutes later I was directing her to Hunter's house. When Hilary parked behind Hunter's car, I said, "I'm having trouble with this one section. Is it okay if I stay for a minute so he can explain it to me?"

"Take your time," Hilary said. She clicked on the radio and closed her eyes, leaning back against the headrest.

"Thanks," I said, and hopped out of the car. Up on the porch I rang the doorbell, and after a moment it was answered by an older man I didn't know. Oh, this had to be Hunter's dad—I'd heard he'd come back from Canada to live with him. He didn't look much like Hunter—almost too old to be his real dad.

"You're a witch," he said after a moment, startling me.

"Uh—" I was caught off guard. No one had ever sensed this before. Including me.

"I get a strange reading off of you," he said, squinting at me. He had a slightly different accent from Hunter, too.

"Da," came Hunter's voice, and then I saw him push in next to his father. "Oh, hullo, Alisa. Are you all right? Did you come here alone?" He looked out past me to the dark yard.

"My stepmother-to-be drove me," I said, feeling an attack of shyness and regret sweeping over me. "I really need to talk to you."

"Sure. Come on in." Hunter turned to his father. "Da, this is Alisa Soto. She's a high school student, part of Kithic."

I noticed that Hunter looked as bad as Morgan had this afternoon. It was as if all the witches I knew had, like, witch pneumonia or something.

Mr. Niall looked at Hunter. "What's going on? Who is she? Why does she feel strange?"

"Calm down, Da," Hunter said. "She might feel different to you because she's only half witch."

I felt like a microbe, the way his dad looked at me.

"But she has power—I can feel it. How is that possible?" he asked.

Hunter shrugged. "Here she stands. So what can I do for you, Alisa?"

Unfortunately, I hadn't planned what to say. So what came out was, "Hunter, what's going on? Why do you and Morgan look like death? Why won't she tell me what's happening?"

"I'm off," Mr. Niall muttered abruptly, and left the room. Strange dad behavior.

I turned back to Hunter, aware that Hilary was waiting outside. "Hunter, what's the deal?" I asked again.

He looked uncomfortable, then ran one hand through his short blond hair, giving himself bed head. "How do you feel?" he asked.

I stared at him. Why did everyone keep asking me that? "I have a headache! *What is going on?*"

"Alisa, there's a dark wave coming to Widow's Vale," he said gently. "Do you know what that is?"

A what? "No."

"It's—a wave, a force, of destruction," Hunter said. "It's dark magick, a spell that a witch or a group of witches casts. They aim it at a particular village or coven, and basically it wipes everything out."

This was too much to take in. I wasn't following. "What are you *talking* about?"

"It's a bad spell," Hunter said simply. "Very uncommon. In the Wiccan world it's rare to come upon someone who practices dark magick. But dark witches can cast a spell when they want to kill other witches, destroy a whole coven, even level a whole village."

I stared at him. "What . . . what . . ." What he was saying sounded like the plot of a Bruce Willis movie—not something that could happen in Widow's Vale. But at the same time, I felt in my bones that he was telling the truth. I didn't understand it, but I did suddenly believe that something bad was coming. Something very bad. "Is this why you and Morgan are sick?"

Hunter nodded. "I would guess your headache is caused by it, too, but since you're half and half, it's not wrecking you as much." He went on to explain what he and Morgan had figured out and also what his father was trying to do, how he was trying to come up with a spell to disperse a dark wave. And he told me that the witch who cast this spell would probably die and that his father was going to be the one who cast it. I felt shocked. Hunter looked really grim, and I couldn't imagine what he was feeling.

"I guess you guys are pretty sure about all this," I said faintly.

He nodded. "It's a situation that's been developing for a while."

"Are you sure your dad—"

"Yes. I'd like for someone else to do it, obviously. But any blood witch is likely to die, and he won't let that happen to someone else."

"And a nonwitch can't cast it?"

"No. They have to be able to summon power. But if they're strong enough to summon power, then they're strong enough to be decimated by the dark wave." He looked frustrated. I felt so sorry for him. If only there was some alternative—a way for a witch to cast the spell yet not be susceptible to the powers of the dark wave. Like if a person were . . .

I frowned as an awful, horrifying thought seeped into my brain. Immediately I shut it down.

"I have to go," I said quickly. "My stepmonster-to-be is waiting for me."

Hunter nodded and opened the door for me.

"The rest of Kithic doesn't know about this," he reminded me. "They wouldn't be able to help, and there's no use in terrifying them."

"Okay." I looked back at him, framed in his doorway. Then I turned and ran down the stairs, to where Hilary was waiting in the car. I was actually really happy to see her.

I had always thought people exaggerated when they talked about sleepless nights. But that night I had one. Every time I felt myself drifting off, I thought, *Great, great, I'm going to sleep.* And of course as soon as I thought that, I was wide awake again. I heard my dad come home after I had gone to bed. I heard Hilary ask him if he wanted something to eat. I remembered how, before Hilary came, I used to leave him something for his dinner when he had late meetings. For twelve years it had been me and him and a succession of housekeepers. By the time I was ten, I'd been able to make dinner by myself, do laundry, and plan a week's worth of meals. I'd thought I was doing pretty damn well, but now I'd been replaced.

After they went to bed, the house was still but not quiet. I listened to the heat cycle on and off, the wind outside pressing against the windows, the creak of the wooden floorboards. Don't think about it, I told myself. Don't think about it. Just go to sleep. But again and again my mind teased the idea out of me: I was half witch. I might be able to call on the power, enough to cast the spell against the dark wave. And I was half not witch. So I might very well be able to survive the dark wave itself.

Don't think about it. Just go to sleep.

I thought about Hunter's weird dad, about him dying right in front of Hunter.

I thought about my mother, whose powers had scared her so much that she had stripped herself of them so that she couldn't cast any kind of spell, good or bad. Had that been the right thing to do? Would I want to do that?

I couldn't control my powers. Sometimes I broke things and made freaky stuff happen. I'd only just found out about being half witch—I didn't even know how I felt about it yet. It scared me; it pissed me off. Then I remembered some of the things I'd seen Morgan do. Now that I knew that *I* was the one who in fact had been causing the scary stuff to happen, I tried to separate out what had been Morgan. She had turned a ball of blue witch fire into flowers, real flowers, raining down on us. Mary K. thought she had saved their aunt's girlfriend from dying after she'd fallen and hit her head. She had come to visit me in the hospital when I had been sick. And I'd gotten better, right away. Those were good things, right?

I hadn't asked to be half witch. I didn't want to be. But since I was, I needed to decide what to do with myself. Was I going to strip myself of my powers, like my mom, and just keep being a regular human, not tuned into the magick that existed all around me? Or was I going to try to be a Morgan, learning all I could, deciding what to do with it, maybe deciding to be a healer? Or was I going to be a total weenie and pretend none of this was happening?

Hunter was about to lose his dad, to watch him die. He didn't have the luxury of pretending none of this was happening.

My brain wound in circles all night, and when I realized that my room was growing lighter with the early dawn, I still didn't have any answers.

"Alisa." Hunter looked surprised to see me on his front porch, and frankly, I felt surprised to be there again. I'd taken a bus most of the way, then walked the rest, the cold wind whipping through my ski jacket. The school day had been endless, and after my sleepless night it had been especially painful to do laps around the gym.

"Come on in," he said. "It's nasty out there."

Inside, my hands twisted together nervously. "I could do it," I said fast, getting the words out before I lost my nerve.

Hunter looked at me blankly. "Do what?"

"I could cast the dark wave spell." I licked my lips. "I'm half and half. Witch enough to cast the spell. Unwitch enough to survive it. I'm your best hope."

I had never seen Hunter speechless—usually he seemed unflappable. Behind him, I saw Mr. Niall come out from the circle room. He saw me and Hunter standing there and came over. Hunter still hadn't said anything. I repeated my offer, talking to Mr. Niall this time.

"You'll die if you cast the dark wave spell. I probably won't. I don't know how strong I am, but I can shatter small appliances from twenty feet," I said, trying for some lame humor. "All of you guys are sick—you look terrible and you can hardly move. All I have is a headache. You need me."

"Nonsense," said Mr. Niall gruffly. "It's out of the question."

"There's no way, Alisa," Hunter said finally. "You're completely untrained, uninitiated. There's no way of knowing if you could do it or not. There's no way we could risk it."

"You can't risk *not* using me," I said. "What if your dad is overcome by the dark wave before he finishes the spell? What happens then? Do you guys even *have* a backup plan?"

From the quick glances they exchanged, I figured they didn't.

"But Alisa," said Hunter, "you've never even cast a spell. This is incredibly difficult and complicated magick. There's no way you could ever learn it in time. Plus we just don't know how strong you are."

"I'm no Morgan, I know that," I said. "I'm not a prodigy. But I know I have *some* powers, from all the weird telekinetic stuff that's happened. I mean, I know I'm the one who's been causing all the weird poltergeisty stuff. I have *some* kind of power. I know the spell would be complicated. But what other choice do you have?"

"I can choose not to send an uninitiated half witch to her death," said Mr. Niall.

"Okay." I met his eyes. "Can you choose to send the rest of Kithic to their deaths because you couldn't see other options?"

Hunter and his father exchanged glances again. "Excuse us," Hunter said abruptly, and taking his father by the arm, he led him into the next room. They were gone almost ten minutes. It felt like ten hours. When they came back, they both looked wary but as if an agreement had been reached.

"My father is going to do some basic testing of your

powers," Hunter told me. "Based on that, we think it might not be the worst idea for you to at least study parts of the spell. We're not completely convinced that you could take part in this, but it won't hurt anything to have you know some of it. As you said, the fact that you're only half witch works in your favor here."

I nodded. Now that they had agreed, a whole new set of fears crossed my mind. But I wasn't able to back out now. My mother had been afraid of her powers and in the end had destroyed them. I wasn't there—not yet. I needed more information; I needed to explore their possibilities first. If I did have real powers and I could somehow learn to harness them, use them for good—well, that would be better than not having any powers at all.

9.
Morgan

><"There can be great power in darkness. There
can be great ecstasy in power."
—Selene Belltower, New York, 1999><

Wednesday. Today sucked. I feel like I have the flu, but
nothing I take makes any difference. I've tried every kind
of sinus medicine I could find—nothing touches how I
feel. Mom has noticed how yucky I look, even for me,
and keeps feeling my forehead. But I have no fever. Just
this horrible, ill feeling that seems to be eating at me from
inside out. I'm so tired of feeling this way—I keep
bursting into tears. Our situation is so dire that I can't
even fully wrap my head around it. I'm trying to go to
school, to eat dinner with my family, to go on as normal,
and all the time I'm trying not to think about the fact that
I and everyone I love might be dead in a week.

In terms of my studies, I worked on some of the

correspondences that Bethany assigned. I'm studying the different structures of crystals and how their individual molecular patterns can aid or deter their powers when used in actual spells. I like this kind of stuff. It's sciency. I'm just finding it hard to think.

On Thursday, I opened my Book of Shadows to write the day's entry. I'd been trying to write a little every day, at least a few sentences about what I was doing, Wicca-wise, what I was focusing on. I realized my brain just wasn't functioning. I needed a Diet Coke. Downstairs, I heard the TV on in the family room. I got my soda from the fridge and poked my head in on my way back upstairs. Dad was working on the computer, Mary K. was on the floor, an open textbook in front of her, and Mom was on the couch, going over new real estate listings while she watched TV. My whole family might be dead in a week; this house might no longer exist; these three people who had been the only family I'd known, who had taken care of me and gotten mad at me and loved me—they might be killed. Because of Ciaran. Because of me. Through no fault of their own. Their only crime being to have adopted and loved me.

Feeling wretched, guilty, and sick, I went upstairs. I wanted to cry but knew that would only make me feel worse. It wasn't just my family. It was Hunter, the person I loved as much as my family. The person I felt so close to, so in love with, whom I wanted so desperately. The thought of him dead, lifeless and charred on the ground, made me feel like I was going to throw up.

And if by some miracle Mr. Niall managed to avert the dark wave, then what? He would still be dead. We would all be alive, but I would have indirectly caused the death of my boyfriend's father. Would Hunter ever be able to forgive me for that? Knowing him, probably. But would I ever be able to forgive myself?

I sat down at my desk, my head in my hands. My birth father was going to take Hunter's father away, just as Hunter had found him again. What could I do? A series of crazy thoughts went through my head. Could I shape-shift into a wolf and kill Ciaran? I didn't think so—I didn't know how to shape-shift by myself. The last time Ciaran had told me what to say and do. Plus I never wanted to shape-shift again—it had been too scary. Plus I didn't think I could really kill anyone, even Ciaran. Could I somehow warn Kithic and their families so they would leave the area? Again, I didn't think so. It would be virtually impossible to convince anyone, and it would only delay the dark wave, not dismantle it. I wondered if I could put a binding spell on Mr. Niall so he couldn't do the spell. Well, if he didn't do the spell, we would all die. On the other hand, since we would all be dead, Hunter wouldn't have to face his father's death.

Then it came to me—an idea that had been fluttering around my mind. I had been ignoring it, but it would be ignored no longer. I could confront Ciaran again. I could tell him that I would join him. A cold feeling settled over me like a mantle. No—it would be lying, and he would see through it. But maybe . . . maybe I could confront him again and then somehow use his true name against him? Maybe I could bind him, shut him down so he couldn't do the final part of the dark wave spell? Ciaran was impossibly strong, but I knew that I had an unusual strength myself. For the most part, I was untrained and uneducated, but I had always been able to call on the power when I needed to. And I had Ciaran's true name. I had discovered it in the middle of our shape-shifting spell. A witch's true name is made of song and color and rune and symbol, all at once. Everything has a true name— rock and tree and wind and bird. Animal, flower, star, river. Witch. To know something's true name is to have ultimate power over it—it can deny you nothing.

And I knew Ciaran's. Of course, he knew I knew it and would be on his guard. But it was a risk I felt I should take.

Looking up, my glance fell on my open textbook. I had a plan.

I waited until I sensed that everyone in the house was asleep. I could feel Mary K. in her room, sleeping deeply and innocently. My dad was sleeping more lightly, but I knew that soon he would go deeper and start snoring. Mom slept as she always did, or at least always had since I'd started notic- ing—with the efficient, light sleep of a mom who manages to get her rest while at the same time being poised for action in case she hears the unmistakable sound of a child crying or throwing up. Mary K. and I were in high school, but Mom would probably sleep that way until we left for college.

I crept out of bed and shut myself in my walk-in closet. In there I drew a small circle on the floor with chalk. I closed myself into the circle, then sat cross-legged and meditated. This circle would increase my powers and give me an added layer of protection. I had no idea where Ciaran was, but I had a feeling he was still nearby. I summoned as much power as I could and sent a concentrated message: *Father—I need you. Power sink.*

I felt a pang of guilt over calling him Father—especially when my real father was sleeping across the hall. I found Ciaran extremely compelling and charismatic, and the idea that he was a blood relation still confused me. For him, I was the child most like him, the one he wanted most to teach. Yet we both despised aspects of each other, and we had never really trusted each other.

I dismantled the circle, feeling sick and tired and close to tears. What was I doing? This had seemed like a good idea an hour ago, but now the whole concept frightened me. I didn't know which outcome would scare me more: that he wouldn't answer my message or that he would. I crawled back into bed, every muscle aching, and lay there in a tense half sleep for I don't know how long. Then it came to me, Ciaran's voice in my mind: *One hour.*

An hour can fly by (when I'm with Hunter) or crawl by (when I'm at school). After I got Ciaran's message, each second seemed to take an entire minute to tick past. After lying stiffly in bed for twenty minutes as if I had rigor mortis, I couldn't stand it any longer. I pulled on some jeans and a hoodie sweatshirt, whisked my hair into a long braid, and, holding my shoes, crept downstairs.

Outside, I buttoned up my coat and pulled on a knit watch cap. Everything felt tight, surreal as I crunched over the spring frost to Das Boot. I felt like I had infrared vision: I could see every tiny movement of every twig on every tree. The moonlight as it filtered through the tree branches was pale and fragile. I opened the car door, put it in neutral, then took off the parking brake. My Valiant began to roll heavily backward toward the street, and soon we bumped almost silently over the curb. I cut the wheel sharply to the left. When I was facing forward, I eased up on the brake again and let myself roll slowly downhill about thirty yards. Then I started the engine, flipped on the headlights and the heater, and headed for the power sink.

When I was younger, I was afraid of the dark. At seventeen, I was more afraid of things like becoming irreversibly evil or of having my soul taken from me by force. The dark didn't seem that bad.

Since I had first started realizing I had witch powers, my magesight had developed, and now I could see quite easily with no light. I parked my car on the road's shoulder and left it unlocked. Every detail stood out as my boots crunched over frost-rimed pine needles, decaying leaves, and water-logged twigs. I was more than twenty minutes early. Casting my senses out, I felt only sleeping animals and birds and the occasional owl or bat. No witch, no Ciaran.

The power sink was in the middle of the graveyard, and to me it felt like every age-worn headstone had something or someone hiding behind it. Ruthlessly I clamped down on my fear, relying on my senses instead of my emotions. I was cold, whipped by a wet, icy wind, but more than that, I was chilled through with fear. No, the dark didn't bother me, but the worst things that had happened in my life had all happened in the last four months, and they had mostly been caused by the man I was waiting to meet. My birth father.

I paced back and forth, and slowly I became aware of tendrils of power beneath me in the earth, tingling energy lines of the power leys that had been there since the beginning of time. They were beneath my feet; they had fed this place for centuries. Their power was in the trees, in the dirt, in the stones, in everything around me.

"Morgan."

I spun around, my heart stopping cold. Ciaran had appeared with no warning: my senses hadn't picked up on even a ripple in the energy around me.

"I was surprised to get your call," he said in that lilting Scottish accent. His hazel eyes seemed to glow at me in the darkness. Slowly I felt the heavy thudding of my heart start up again. "I hope you called me here to make me happy—to tell me that we're going to be the most remarkable witches the world has ever seen."

I felt so many things, looking at him. Anger, regret, fear, confusion, and even, I was ashamed to admit it—love? Almost admiration? He was so powerful, so focused. He had no uncertainty in his life: his path was clear. I envied that.

I didn't have an exact plan—first I needed to know for sure what his plans were.

"I've been feeling awful," I told him. "Is it from the dark wave?"

"Aye, daughter," he said, sounding regretful. "If you know far enough in advance, you can protect yourself from the illness. But if you don't . . ." Which explained why he looked bright eyed and bushy tailed, but I felt like I was going to throw up or collapse. "I can do a lot to help your symptoms," he went on. "And then the next time you'll be protected before it starts."

"I'm not joining you," I said, drawing cold air into my lungs.

"Then why did you call me here?" There was a chill underlying his tone that was far worse than that of the night air.

"My way isn't your way," I said. "It isn't a path I can choose. Why can't you just let me be? I'm a nobody. Kithic is nothing. You don't need to destroy us. We can't do anything to hurt you."

"Kithic is nothing," he agreed, his voice like smoke rising off water. He stepped closer to me, so close I could almost touch him. "An amateurish circle of mediocre kids. But you, my dear—you are not nothing. You possess the power to devastate anything in your path—or to create unimaginable beauty."

"No, I don't," I objected. "Why do you think that? I'm not even initiated—"

"You just don't understand, do you?" he said sharply. "You don't understand who you are, *what* you are. You're the last witch of Belwicket. You're my daughter. You're the sgiùrs dàn."

"The what?" I felt hysteria rising in me like nausea.

"The fated scourge. The destroyer."

"The *what?*" I repeated in a squeak.

"The signs say that it's you, Morgan," he explained. "The destroyer comes every several generations to change the course of her clan. This time it's you who will change the course of the Woodbanes—just as your great ancestor Rose did centuries ago. So you see, you have more power than you realize. And I simply can't let that power be in opposition to my own. It would be . . . foolish of me to go against fate."

"You're insane," I breathed.

He grinned then, his teeth shining whitely in the night. "No, Morgan. Ambitious, yes. Insane, no. It's all true. Just ask the Seeker. At any rate, you won't be around long enough for it to really matter. Either you join me now or you die."

I stared at him, seeing a reflection of my face in his more masculine features. "You wouldn't really kill me." Please don't do this, I begged silently. Please.

A look of pain crossed his face. "I don't want to. But I will." He sounded regretful. "I must. If I have to choose your life or mine, I'll choose mine."

Hearing him confirm this broke my heart. I felt a sadness in my chest like a dull weight. Any of the confused affection I had for him, any lingering hopes I had of someday, somehow having an actual relationship with the man who had fathered me, dissipated. A real father would never hurt his own daughter—as a real soul mate wouldn't have killed his lover. Ciaran was failing on all counts.

With no warning I was overtaken by a wave of rage, at his arrogance, his selfishness, his shortsightedness. He would rather kill me than know me! He would rather wipe out an entire coven than achieve his ends in other ways! He was a bully and a coward, hiding behind a dark wave that had killed countless innocent people. He was going to kill me because I—a teenager, an unschooled witch—scared him. I didn't think before I moved. Suddenly I felt like I was on a playground and being picked on. I flung out my fist, catching him squarely on the shoulder. Taken by surprise, as I was, Ciaran caught my wrist in his hand, and then I was twisted down to the ground, crying out. This wasn't magick—this was just a man who was stronger than me. But then he muttered something and I felt a horrible stillness coming over me, a remote coldness that I had felt once before, when Cal had put a binding spell on me.

Dammit! My mind raced ahead in panic as I knelt, so numb I couldn't feel the dampness of the ground seeping through my jeans. What had I been thinking? I knew Ciaran's true name! But instead of using it, I had lashed out like a stupid kid!

He released my hand and stepped back, looking angry and concerned. "What is this about, Morgan?" he said, sounding, ironically, quite fatherly. I couldn't form words—it was like being under anesthesia, those scary minutes before you go totally out. My brain felt wrapped in damp cotton, synapses firing slowly and erratically. I couldn't move; I no longer felt like I had a body. Besides sheer panic, I was now filled with anger. Could I be any stupider? Magick is all about clarity of thought. Clarity of thought dictates clarity of action. Not thinking, lashing out blindly, not having a firm plan and sticking to it, not only meant trouble—for me, now, it meant death.

I'm not one of those heroine-type people who think best under pressure. Mostly, under pressure, I just want to cry. I wanted to cry now. I was choked with frustration, with fury, with fear. Instead I knelt on the cold ground, my father standing before me, holding my life in his hands like an egg.

"Morgan." He sounded surprised, disappointed. "What are you thinking? Are you really going up against *me*? I'm much stronger than you are."

My mouth moved, but I couldn't form words. *Then why are you so scared of me?* I thought, sending him the message.

I wondered if I could just *think* his true name—if that would work. Probably not. I was reluctant to try. If he even knew it was in my mind, I'd be toast. I had already made one terrible, possibly fatal mistake. Anything I did from now on would have to be a sure step.

Foggily, my eyes went to Ciaran's face. He was talking to me in a low tone, and I struggled to understand what he was saying. "Would it be so terrible to join me? Am I such a monster? I'm your father. I could teach you things that would make you cry at their beauty, their perfection. Do you really want to throw this opportunity away?"

My eyes were focused on him as he spoke. Think, think, I told myself dreamily. Think or he'll win. A binding spell was one of the odder spells one could be under. There were different levels of it—from simply being unable to harm another being to being virtually comatose. The way I felt now was like being wrapped in many layers of tissue: hard to get out of, yet made of thin, tearable layers. I also knew that keeping me in this spell required Ciaran's concentration. One could work a binding spell from a distance, but he hadn't had time for that. This was a quick one, hastily put together and requiring his continued effort.

If I broke his concentration, if he for one millisecond dropped his guard, I might be able to do something. Like whimper pathetically and then fall over. Or break free. And then use his true name. It was just so hard to *think*. I could barely move my eyes—that was all. What were my options? I didn't think I could send a witch message while I was bound. I couldn't form the sounds of Maeve's power chant. What could I do? What was I capable of? Starting fires was something I was good at—but everything around me seemed damp. Could I set wet leaves on fire?

Ciaran was talking, pacing back and forth, earnestly trying to convince me why black equaled white. My eyes followed him, but he didn't look at me much: he was sure I couldn't break free.

Fire. Heat. Heat plus dampness . . . made steam. Steam could be powerful. Most heavy machinery used to be run on steam. Radiators.

Then it came to me. With great effort, I slowly slid my gaze past Ciaran to the trunk of a pine tree. Heat, I thought. Heat and water. Heat. Fire. I imagined sparks, tiny flames flickering into being, fire warming bark, running beneath it. Ciaran didn't notice the very faint ribbon of steam coming from the tree behind him. His soliloquy continued, as if he thought that if he talked long enough, I would finally be convinced.

Heat, building beneath the pine bark. Pressure building. Cells expanding. Tiny fissures splitting wood fibers. The water in every cell evaporating, turning to steam. I lost myself in it, imagining that I could see the bark swelling, feel the fibers splitting, feel the pressure building.

Crack!

With the force of a small explosion, chunks of pine bark flew outward, hitting Ciaran, almost hitting me. He whirled, his hand outstretched, ready to deflect an attack, but it took him several seconds to see where the sound had come from. Seconds in which his concentration was weakened. In those precious seconds I made a tremendous effort and managed to work my right arm. Summoning every bit of power in me, I raised my voice to say his true name. He whirled as the notes began, my voice sounding dull and leaden under the binding spell. My right hand clumsily sketched runes in the air, and with a last breath I managed to complete it—his true name, a color and song and rune all at once.

He hissed something at me, but I held up my hand and deflected it.

Teeth gritted, I said, "Take off the binding spell."

The look of fury and horror on his face was frightening, even though I knew I had power over him.

"Take it off!"

His arm raised against his will, and words fell from his lips. In moments I could take deep breaths, and when the spell dissolved, I fell to my hands and knees.

"Morgan, don't make this kind of mistake," Ciaran said softly. But he wasn't in control anymore.

"Be quiet," I panted, slowly standing up, rubbing feeling back into my arms and legs. The cold of the night air made me shake: I had been motionless for too long.

I looked at him, my biological father, an extremely powerful witch whom I had both reluctantly admired and truly feared. He had put a binding spell on me! He had planned to kill me, kill my friends, my family. I let my contempt show in my face as I looked at him.

"Ciaran of Amyranth," I said, my lungs still feeling stiff, my tongue thick, "I have power over you. I have your true name, and you are bidden to do my will." I was trying to remember the exact phrasing from various witch texts. His eyes flashed, but he stood quietly before me. "You will never hurt me again," I said strongly. I wasn't sure exactly how a true name worked—but I felt that pretty much anything I said went. "Do you understand?"

His lips were pressed tightly together.

"Say it," I said, feeling unreal, giving him orders.

"I will never hurt you again." It looked like the words were costing him.

With quick, efficient motions I put a binding spell on him, just to be safe. He stood in the darkness like a handsome mannequin, but fire was burning in his eyes and his gaze never left me. "I have your true name," I said again for good measure. "You have no power."

I backed away from him, feeling exhausted. My watch said 2:26 A.M. Pressing one hand against my temple, keeping my eyes open, I sent out a witch message as strongly as I knew how. *Hunter. Power sink. Now. Bring your dad. I need you.*

10.
Alisa

><"The secret of a successful dark wave is in creating its limitations. Be clear in your intent, unemotional. Act because of a calm, logical decision—not out of anger or revenge."

—Ciaran MacEwan, Scotland, 2000 ><

"No, no—it's nal nithrac, not nal bithdarc," Mr. Niall said, not bothering to hide his irritation.

I gritted my teeth. "Isn't there a nal bithdarc in there somewhere?"

"There's a bith dearc," Hunter reminded me. "But not till a bit later."

I let out a breath and sank down onto the wooden floor in front of the fireplace. It was way freaking late, I was exhausted, I had a headache, and I was kind of hungry. "Is there any cake left?" I asked.

Hunter had made a killer pound cake yesterday, and we'd all been wolfing it down in between them teaching me this wretched horrible spiteful spell. Without a word Hunter went into the kitchen and came back with a slab of cake on a plate. I picked it up with my fingers and took a bite.

Mr. Niall sat on the floor next to me and held his hands out to the fire. He looked like death warmed over, gray skinned and hollow eyed. Starting last Tuesday night, he'd been working with me on the spell to fight the dark wave. Dad and Hilary thought I was working on my science project with Mary K. I had told Dad I'd be home late, and he agreed. Another sign of Hilary's turning my dad crazy: A year ago he'd never have let me stay out past his bedtime.

I looked at my watch: past midnight. And I had to go to school tomorrow. Thank God tomorrow was Friday. I could sleepwalk through classes, then go home and crash. Then come here and not have to worry about getting up the next morning.

"I'm sorry," I said, trying not to spray crumbs. "This is all new to me."

"I know," said Mr. Niall, rubbing the back of his head. "And this is a hard one. Most witches start with spells to keep flies away, things like that."

"Keep flies away," I mused. "I could probably handle something like that."

Hunter gave a dry laugh, then headed back to the kitchen when the teakettle began whistling.

He came back with three mugs. It was hot and sweet, laced with honey and lemon. I waited till Mr. Niall had drunk his, then tiredly got to my feet. "Okay. Can we start right at the beginning of the second part, where we do the sigils?"

"Lass—" Mr. Niall hesitated. "You've been trying, but—"

"But what? But I keep messing up? It's late, I'm tired, this is my first dark wave spell," I said testily. "I know I need lots more practice. That's why I'm here." My jaw jutted out, and I realized that I had some pride invested here. I *wanted* to be able to do this. Not to look good in front of Hunter and his dad, but because I was my mother's daughter. She'd come from a whole line of witches, yet she'd been so freaked out by her powers that she'd stripped herself of them. That seemed kind of cowardly to me. My powers scared me, too, but it seemed so wrong to give up like that. I felt like, I'm me, *I'm* in control of me. My powers were not in control of me. Doing the spell was a crash course in learning to channel my powers. So far it hadn't been that successful: there had been several times when I'd been so upset or frustrated that I'd popped a lightbulb overhead, caused a stack of firewood to topple (I assumed that had been me), and made a framed picture drop off the wall.

Those were the kinds of things that had scared me about Morgan and her powers—the whole idea of her being out of control. But it *hadn't* been her, and I had to live with that part of me. I needed to get it together. The weird thing was, by the time the third thing had happened (I was almost screaming in frustration after doing a whole set of sigils perfectly—but backward), Hunter and his dad started to find it funny. Funny! Stuff that had made me quit Kithic and run a mile from Morgan—made me dislike her, mistrust her. Now, after spending so many hours with me in this house, they had started making a big show of throwing out their hands to catch things—vases, lamps, mugs—every time I even raised my voice. It was like that scene in *Mary Poppins* where the admiral sets off his cannon and everyone runs to their posts.

"Look at yourselves," I said, not meanly. "You guys can

hardly eat, hardly sleep. The dark wave coming is draining you. I'm the picture of health next to you. This is still a good plan. Which means you still have to teach me."

Looking defeated, Mr. Niall stood up, and we both faced west with our arms out.

"Give me the words," he said.

Concentrating, I tried to let the spell come to me instead of reaching out to grab it. "An de allaigh, ne rith la," I half sang. "Bant ne tier gan, ne rith la." And so on it went, the words of limitation that were the second part of the spell. After one more phrase Mr. Niall and I started moving together, like synchronized swimmers. My right hand came out and traced three runes, then a sigil, a rune, and two more sigils. These would focus the spell and add power. Each rune stood not only for itself, but also for a word that began with its sound. Each word had meaning and added to the spell.

I crossed my arms over my chest, palms down, each hand on a shoulder. Standing tall, I continued, "Sgothrain, tal nac, nal nithrac, bogread, ne rith la."

Ten minutes later I sounded the last part of the second stage of the spell. I wanted to drop onto the floor and sleep right there for the rest of my life. But when I looked up and saw admiration on Hunter's face and a reserved approval on Mr. Niall's, I felt a rush of energy.

"Was that okay?" I asked, knowing that they would have stopped me if it wasn't.

"That was fine, Alisa," said Mr. Niall. "That was good. If we can get the other parts down as well, we'll be in good shape."

I tried not to groan out loud: there were three other parts to the spell. The whole thing took almost an hour to perform.

"I felt your power," Hunter said. "Did you feel it?"

I nodded. "Yes. It seems to be getting stronger—or maybe I'm just better at recognizing it. It's still so new to me. Is it weird for a half witch to have power?"

Hunter shrugged. "It's an exceedingly rare condition, right, Da?"

"Very rare. I don't think I've ever met another half witch, let alone one that had powers," Mr. Niall said. "I've heard stories—but usually a female witch can't conceive by an ordinary male. And when a male witch conceives with a nonwitch female, their child is always relatively powerless."

Heat flushed my cheeks. I really didn't want to think about my parents conceiving anything.

"I wonder, though," said Mr. Niall. "I wonder if your having powers, or this level of powers, has anything to do with your mother stripping herself of hers. Stripping yourself of powers is rather like getting plastic surgery: on the outside, you appear different, but your genes are the same. *Your* nose looks different, but you have the ability to pass on your old nose to your offspring. The fact that your mother stripped herself of her powers didn't in any way mean she was no longer a blood witch, with the capability of passing her strength, her family's strength, on to her offspring." He frowned at me. "But you do have a high level of power, even assuming that you inherited your genetic due from your mother. Most half witches are relatively weak because they get power from only one side of the family. But you . . ."

"I break things," I supplied.

Mr. Niall chuckled—a rare occurrence. "Well, there's that, lass. No, I was getting at the fact that you seem to have as much power as a full blood witch. I wonder if it's possible that because your mother stripped herself, her powers were somehow concentrated in you."

Hunter looked curious. "You mean Alisa has not only her own powers as a half witch, but her mother's powers as a full witch."

Mr. Niall looked at me and nodded slowly. "Yes," he said. "It's something I've never seen before, but I suppose that's what I mean."

"You don't have brothers or sisters, right, Alisa?" Hunter asked.

I shook my head. "Except for the half sibling that's due in six months. But it wouldn't have any witch at all."

"It would have been interesting if you had, to see what their powers would be like," he said.

"Yeah. I'm a walking science experiment," I said tartly. "I mean, do you think I could ever learn to control my power, all the telekinetic stuff?"

Hunter's father nodded. "Yes—I can't think of any reason why you wouldn't be able to. It would be a skill to learn, like any other skill. It would take practice, commitment, and time, but I feel sure it could be done."

"Okay," I said with a sigh. "I guess I'll start on that as soon as this dark wave thing is over."

Hunter and Mr. Niall met glances over my head, and in a flash I got what they were thinking: that if we couldn't some-how combat the dark wave, I wouldn't ever have to worry about my telekinetic stuff again. Because I would be dead.

Hunter stretched again, then frowned slightly and went still. I listened for any unusual sounds but didn't hear any-thing or see anything out of place.

"What, lad?" asked Mr. Niall, and Hunter held up a finger for silence.

"It's Morgan," he said then, getting to his feet.

"What, outside?" I asked, thinking he had sensed her coming up.

"No. At the power sink. She wants me to come there." He looked at his father. "She said to bring you."

Without discussion they walked into the front room and pulled on their coats.

Halfway out the door Hunter asked, "Do you want me to give you a ride home?"

I looked around the room at Mr. Niall's spell books, Rose's Book of Shadows, and my scrawled notes on endless messy pieces of paper. I needed more practice. "No thanks— I'll wait here, if that's okay. I'll go over the third part of the spell again."

Hunter considered it for a moment, then nodded. "Right, then. But stay close to a phone, and if anything weird happens, call nine-one-one."

"Okay." Anything weird? 911? What was going on?

Then they were gone, and I was alone. It was almost two-thirty in the morning. I put another thin log on the fire in the circle room and began to work through the forms again.

11.
Morgan

After ten minutes of holding Ciaran in a binding spell, I began
to feel that I should have let him sit down first. Because I felt
a little *guilty* that one of the most evil witches in the last two
centuries, a man responsible for hundreds if not thousands of
deaths, a man who had in fact killed my *mother,* was possibly
getting uncomfortable having to stand still in one place for so
long! I'm so pathetic, I just can't stand myself sometimes.

I was leaning against a headstone, occasionally walking
around to keep warm, when Hunter and his father arrived. I
had never been so glad to see another person in my life. I
felt them get out of Hunter's car; then Hunter led his father
through the woods to the Methodist cemetery. I hurried
forward to meet them.

"Thanks for coming," I said, wrapping my arms around Hunter's waist and leaning my head against his chest for a second. I kept part of my concentration on Ciaran but knew he couldn't budge that binding spell. I'd always been good at them. "Things got a little crazy."

"What's going on?" Hunter held me by my shoulders and looked down into my face with concern.

"Over here." I waved my hand limply toward Ciaran, and Hunter took a few steps before he spotted him. Then he froze, his hands already coming up for ward-evil spells. "He's under a binding spell," I said quickly.

"Goddess," Mr. Niall breathed hoarsely, having spotted Ciaran.

Hunter turned and looked at me like I had suddenly revealed elf wings on my back.

I shook my head, unsure of how to begin. "I just couldn't stand the fact that all this was happening because of me. If I weren't here, Amyranth would have left Kithic alone. I felt like it was all my fault. I decided to contact Ciaran, to try to reason with him."

I glanced at Ciaran and almost shivered at the look in his eyes. He seemed less recognizable, his eyes glittering darkly, with none of the mild affection or warmth that they usually held.

"So you called him to meet you here?" Hunter asked, disbelief in his voice. "And he came?"

"Uh-huh. And he said that if I didn't join him that he would have to take out our coven. Because I was too dangerous to live if I wasn't on his side. Because I was the—the, um, sgiùrs dàn? Something like that. Then he put a binding spell on me—"

"Hold it," Hunter interrupted. "Wait a second. He said you were the sgiùrs dàn?" He looked at Ciaran questioningly, but the older man's face didn't change.

"Yes. Then he put a binding spell on me, and I thought I was going to die, right here, tonight. But I distracted him for a second, and broke his concentration, and managed to put a binding spell on *him*." I rubbed my hand across my forehead, feeling old and sick and tired.

"How did you distract him?" Hunter asked.

I glanced at Mr. Niall—I thought he'd been way too quiet. In the night's darkness he almost glowed with a white rage. He was standing stiffly, hands clenched into fists. He looked like he might attack Ciaran at any moment.

"I created a pocket of steam, under that tree's bark," I explained, pointing. "It made the bark pop off hard, and it distracted Ciaran just enough for me to be able to use my hand and to speak."

"What did you say that got you out of the binding spell?" asked Mr. Niall, his voice hard.

"I said—his true name." The last three words tiptoed out of my mouth. I had never told anyone that I knew Ciaran's true name, and part of me didn't like telling anyone now.

Hunter's eyes got so big, I could see white all around the green irises. His jaw went slack, and then he cocked his head to one side. "Morgan. You said *what?*"

"I said his true name," I repeated. "Then I made him take off the binding spell."

Both Hunter and Mr. Niall looked from me to Ciaran: they had suddenly found themselves in a situation that defied all reason. Ciaran's eyes now seemed as black as the night, and considering that all he could do was blink, he managed to put a lot of scary expression into it.

"And I put a binding spell on him," I finished. "Then I called you. I don't know what to do now."

Just then, with a hoarse cry, Mr. Niall launched himself at Ciaran. Using his shoulder, he butted Ciaran hard in the stomach, then followed him down to the ground and pulled back his fist. I was already on my way to them when Hunter's father landed a hard blow to the side of Ciaran's head. Hunter beat me there and tried to pull his father off, but finally it took both of us to drag Mr. Niall away.

"Da, stop it," Hunter panted, pinning his father down with one knee. "This isn't the time or the place. Get ahold of yourself."

"I'm going to kill him," Mr. Niall spat, and I got angry.

"No, you're not!" I snapped. "I understand how you feel, but you don't decide what happens to him. That's the council's job."

"No, not the council." Hunter shook his head. "They've bungled things twice with him already. No—it's up to us. We have to strip him of his powers."

Ciaran lay on the ground like a mummy where he had fallen. He hadn't displayed much response when Mr. Niall had attacked him, but now, at Hunter's words, real fear entered his eyes. I had seen a witch stripped of his powers once, and I'd hoped never to see it again. The idea of seeing it happen to Ciaran was stomach turning. Yet I knew, realistically, that there was no other real option. If we let Ciaran go, he would be exactly the same. He would continue to create the dark wave, killing anything that got in his way. He would always be a threat to me, no matter what kind of promise I could get out of him. Once more I met his gaze and saw the disappointment there, the rage, the regret. I looked away.

"Yeah, you're right," I said roughly, trying not to cry. "I guess you need five witches."

"We have three here," said Hunter. If he was surprised by my acquiescence, he didn't show it.

"I can't do it," I said immediately. "Get someone else."

Hunter took his knee off his dad's chest and warily let him up. Mr. Niall slowly got to his feet and stalked off to lean against a weatherworn headstone. Hunter stood quite still for a couple of minutes, and I knew he was sending witch messages. Without looking at Ciaran's face, I went over and pulled him into a sitting position, awkwardly propping him up. There was a lot I wanted or needed to say to him, but I didn't trust myself to speak. In my heart, I knew we were doing the best thing. After he was sitting up, I sank onto a cement bench nearby and concentrated on the binding spell.

Then we had to wait. Hunter came to sit next to me. I felt like I had been out here about three years and wanted to go home, curl up in my comforter, and cry until dawn.

"Morgan," Hunter said, his voice pitched for me alone. "You never told me that you knew Ciaran's true name."

It was a statement, not a question, but I knew what he wanted.

"I learned it the night we shape-shifted," I said. "It was part of his spell. I don't know why I never told anyone. It just felt—wrong to tell."

"Or maybe you didn't want Ciaran to be that vulnerable to anyone else. Because whatever else he is, he helped make you."

I frowned, not wanting to acknowledge this fact at the moment.

"All this time you knew his true name," Hunter continued, rubbing his chin with one hand. "You could have done anything you wanted with it. You could have killed him, controlled him, turned him in to the council or to me. You could have bound him and done a tàth meànma brach so that you would have all his knowledge, all his skill."

I shook my head. "No—I couldn't have. I couldn't have killed him, and somehow I just kept hoping that he would—be different. And I don't want his knowledge or his skill. I don't want to have anything to do with it."

Hunter nodded. He was sitting close but not touching me, and I wondered how upset he was that I hadn't told him.

It wasn't long before we heard two cars driving up, and moments later we were joined by Alyce Fernbrake, Bethany Malone, and a woman I didn't recognize.

"Where's Finn?" Hunter asked.

"He couldn't come," Alyce said, and the way she said it made me think he just hadn't wanted to come. I didn't blame him. "This is Silver Hennessy."

Awkward introductions were made—we all knew why we were here: he was sitting ten feet away from us. I started to feel queasy and had to sit down again.

"More than five witches can take part," Hunter said to me. "Five is the minimum number."

"I can't," I said, and he didn't press me.

Having to do this particular rite out in the woods, with no advance warning, wasn't ideal. Usually the witch in charge chooses a suitable time and place, where the phase of the moon helps lessen the discomfort or the place feels more protected. Ciaran, because of his very nature, couldn't be held for any length of time. It would be here and now.

Hunter had brought his athame, and now he drew a pentacle on the ground, about eight feet across. The litter of leaves obscured the ground, but he muttered some words and raised his athame high. Then he traced it on the ground, and it left a fine, faintly glowing azure line.

I couldn't bring myself to look at Ciaran, to see the increasing rage and panic on his face. Instead I huddled on my cement bench, my head on my knees. I knew that using his true name had been the right thing to do. I also knew that I would feel badly about doing it for a long, long time. Bethany Malone and Alyce both came and sat next to me, and I felt the warmth of them on each side of me. Bethany put her arm around my shoulders, and Alyce patted my cold knee. I leaned my head against Alyce, grateful she was here. I didn't know Silver Hennessy, but I completely trusted Bethany and Alyce and knew that Ciaran was lucky they were performing the rite.

Mr. Niall stood close to Hunter, as if watching to make sure he was setting the rite up correctly. Occasionally they murmured to each other. Mr. Niall refused to look at Ciaran or me, but I felt that he was trying to release some of his own fury and pain. He would need a clear head to participate in this.

Soon Alyce left me and went to sit by Ciaran with Silver. Alyce was just about the gentlest, least judgmental person I had ever known, but the look she gave Ciaran was reserved and sad. I knew that Ciaran must be feeling incredibly sore and stiff by now, but of course I couldn't lessen the binding spell. And this was nothing compared to how he would feel an hour from now. Not that he didn't deserve it. Every once in a while I felt a rough growl in my mind, as if a trapped animal were trying to break free. It was Ciaran, trying to claw his way through the binding spell.

Sitting there, remembering the last time I had seen this rite, I realized we needed to make some arrangement about Ciaran, for afterward. I left Bethany, went over to Hunter, and waited until he paused and met my eyes.

"I think I should call Killian to come get him," I said very quietly. "None of us is going to want to take care of him afterward."

For long moments Hunter looked at me, then he nodded. "That's good thinking, Morgan. Can you send the message?"

I nodded and went back to sit next to Bethany on my bench, where I concentrated and sent a witch message to my half brother Killian MacEwan, the only one of my half siblings I had met. Despite being extremely different, we had forged a somewhat caring relationship. After tonight, I assumed, that would be over.

When Killian answered me, he was in Poughkeepsie, an hour and a half away. I asked him to come to Widow's Vale at once and told him it was important, but didn't tell him why. He said he would, and I hoped he meant it.

At last Hunter stood. "All right, I think we can begin."

Bethany squeezed my shoulder, stroked my hair briefly, then joined Hunter, Alyce, and Silver as they lifted Ciaran and carried him into the middle of the pentacle. Mr. Niall stayed away—I wondered if he didn't trust himself to get close to Ciaran without attacking him. The four witches bent Ciaran's unresisting body so he was kneeling on the ground with his arms by his sides. Then Hunter ran his hands over Ciaran, taking off anything metal, taking off his shoes, loosening his collar, his cuffs. He was quick and efficient, but not rough. I saw a tiny muscle jerking in Ciaran's cheek. With no warning a sudden, searing pain ripped into my mind. I cried out and pressed my hand to the side of my head. I heard Hunter shout and felt a flash fire of panic in the air around me. In an instant I realized it was Ciaran, trying to break free. Without looking I flung out my hand, singing out Ciaran's true name. The pain in my head dulled, and when I raised my eyes, I saw Ciaran sprawled motionless on his side on the cold ground. He had almost made it. He had almost broken free.

Hunter looked over at me questioningly.

I nodded. "I have him," I said shakily, rubbing the dull ache in my skull.

"Right. One more time," Hunter said, and again he and the women propped Ciaran into a kneeling position. I knew that if I hadn't managed to stop Ciaran so quickly, we'd all be dead now.

Then Hunter stood at the top of the pentacle, and the other four arranged themselves around the points. With closed eyes and bowed heads, each witch concentrated on relaxing, on letting go of emotion, of releasing any anger they might have. After several minutes Hunter raised his head, and I saw that he was a Seeker and no longer just someone I loved.

"East, south, west, and north," he began, "we call on your guardians to help us in this sad rite. Goddess and God, we invoke your names, your spirits, your powers here tonight so that we may act fairly, with justice and compassion. Here, under the full moon of this, the first and last month of the year, we have gathered to take from Ciaran MacEwan his magick and his powers, as punishment for crimes committed against human and witch, woman and man and child. Alyce of Starlocket, are you in agreement?"

"Yes," Alyce said faintly.

"Bethany of Starlocket, are you in agreement?"

"Yes." Her voice was more strong.

"Silver of Starlocket, are you in agreement?"

"Yes."

"Daniel of Turloch-eigh, are you in agreement?"

"Aye." His voice was like a rasp.

"No more shall he wake a witch," Hunter said.

Silver, Alyce, Bethany, and Mr. Niall all repeated, "No more shall he wake a witch."

"No more shall he know the beauty and terror of your power," Hunter said, and they repeated it. I heard it echoing in my mind as I rocked myself back and forth on the cold cement.

"No more shall he do harm to any living thing."

"No more shall he be one of us."

"Ciaran MacEwan, we have met, and in the name of witches everywhere, we have passed judgment on you. You have called on the dark wave, you are responsible for untold deaths, you have participated in other rites of darkness that are abhorrent to those who follow the Goddess. Tonight you will have your powers stripped from you. Do you understand?"

There was no response from Ciaran, but the muffled clawing sensation in my head increased. I raised my voice from where I was. "He's trying to break the binding spell," I said.

"Strengthen it," Hunter said gently, and I closed my eyes and did as he said.

When Hunter had stripped David Redstone of his powers, Sky had used a drumbeat to guide our energy. Tonight the five witches began chanting, first one and then another, and kept time with rhythmic stamping of their feet on the ground. Hunter's voice was deeper and rougher than the women's; Mr. Niall's sounded thinner and weaker. Everyone looked sad. Their voices blended and wove together, but instead of the beautiful, exhilarating power chants I was used to, this one seemed harsh, mournful, more cacophonous. I felt the increasing energy in the air around me; goose bumps broke out on my arms and my hair felt full of static. I could feel that every animal and bird had left the area. I didn't blame them.

When I looked down, I saw that the star, the pentagram, had begun to glow with a whiter light—their energy. I knew what was coming next, and my stomach clenched. I drew my knees up again and held them tightly against myself and felt that I would bear the scars of this night forever. As would Ciaran.

The chanting ended abruptly, and Hunter bent to touch his athame to the white lines of energy. The knife glowed briefly, and when Hunter raised it, it seemed to draw up a pale, whitish blue film, like smoke or cotton candy. Slowly Hunter walked around the pentacle, drawing this light around Ciaran, as if he were at the bottom of a slow, beautiful tornado. When the light reached the top of Ciaran's head, Hunter gave me a sharp look.

"Take off the binding spell."

Praying he knew what he was doing, I released my father. In a split second he sprang up, roaring like a tortured animal, and just as quickly he seemed to hit the barrier of light and drop like a dead thing to the ground, where he lay on his side. He could move now, and his hands clutched at his clothes, at his hair. His bare feet moved convulsively, and he drew in on himself like a snail, trying to avoid any contact with the light. His eyes were closed, his mouth working soundlessly.

A sob erupted from deep within me, then another and another. No longer having to concentrate on holding the spell, my emotions poured out, and I was so shaken and upset that I wasn't even embarrassed. Through my tears I saw glistening traces on Alyce's face, on Bethany's. Silver looked deeply saddened. Mr. Niall looked calm, focused. Hunter looked grim, purposeful, not angry or hateful. Still chanting quietly by himself, he spiraled the energy around Ciaran, slowly and completely. When at last he lifted the athame away, it swirled around Ciaran unaided.

Then the images began, the images that defined who Ciaran had been, who he had become. Watching through my tears, still shaking with sobs, I saw a boy, handsome and happy, running across a green Scottish field with a kite. It was diving groundward, and with a flick of his hand, young Ciaran sent it back up to the clouds. I saw fourteen-year-old Ciaran being initiated, wearing a dark, almost black robe sprinkled with silver threads. He looked very solemn, and I felt that in his eyes there was already a glimmer of the witch he would become. Ciaran aged in the visions, and we saw teenage Ciaran courting girls, working on spells, having arguments with a man I thought must have been his father—my grandfather. Then to my shock, I saw a teenage Ciaran with a young Selene Belltower, just for an instant. I blinked, and there was Ciaran, being wed to Grania, her belly already round with their first child, Kyle. My breath stopped, sobs caught in my throat, as I saw Ciaran with the woman I recognized as Maeve Riordan, my birth mother. Maeve and Ciaran were wrapped tightly together, clinging to each other as if to be separated would equal death. Then Maeve was crying, turning away from him, and Ciaran was staring after her, his hands clenched. I saw Ciaran darkly silhouetted against the bright background of a burning barn. On and on it went, these images being born from the energy and floating upward to disappear into nothingness. On the ground, Ciaran lay jerking as if he were having a seizure, and I could make out a thin keening coming from him.

The images turned darker then, and I flinched as I saw Ciaran performing blood sacrifices, then using spells against other witches who cowered before him in pain. I felt ill as I saw him calling the dark wave, saw the exultation in his face, how he felt the glory of that power as before him whole villages were decimated, the people fleeing pointlessly. It grew to be too much, and I closed my eyes, resting my head on my knees.

When I looked up next, I saw myself and Ciaran hugging, I saw us turning into wolves, and even from over where I was, I felt Alyce's and Silver's surprise. And then we were at tonight, when I had used his true name and he had been bound. When the last image had floated away and no more were coming, I knew that we had seen his life unraveling before us, seen the destruction of everything that had made him who and what he was.

My blood father lay unmoving on the cold March ground. Hunter drew his athame, and slowly the swirling energy surrounded it and seemed to be absorbed by it. When the last of the energy had gone, Hunter sheathed the knife and went to stand over Ciaran.

"Ciaran MacEwan, witch of the Woodbanes, is now ended," Hunter said. "The Goddess teaches us that every ending is also a beginning. May there be a rebirth from this death."

With those words, the rite was over.

When David had been stripped, Hunter had brought him healing tea, and Alyce had held him as he cried. I knew no one would do that for Ciaran. I wanted to go sit next to him, but my guilt was too great. Then Alyce, softly rounded, dressed in her trademark lavender and gray, knelt down on the ground near where Ciaran lay crumpled.

Hunter came and sat next to me on the cement bench, carefully not touching me. He seemed much older than nineteen and looked like he'd been battling a long illness.

Bethany stooped, touched Ciaran's temple once, then came to me and did the same thing. I felt her caring, her concern, and then she left through the woods. Silver Hennessey came to clasp Hunter's hand, then she, too, left, after a sympathetic glance at me.

Mr. Niall strode over to us. "I'm off, lad," he said in his odd, rough voice. "Good work."

I gazed stonily at the ground.

"Morgan," he said, surprising me. "It was a hard thing. But you did right." I didn't look up as he walked away.

Alyce stayed by Ciaran, and Hunter stayed by me. We were all silent. It was past four o'clock in the morning, and I felt that I would never sleep or eat or laugh again.

We sat in the darkness like that for another hour until we heard Killian crashing through the woods, and then he emerged through the cedars and pines.

"Hey, sis," he said cheerfully, and it was clear he'd been drinking. Great—he'd driven here from Poughkeepsie. He ignored Hunter, which wasn't unusual.

"Killian," I whispered. I had no idea what to say—words didn't cover this situation. I motioned over to where Ciaran lay on the ground.

If I had seen my real father, Sean Rowlands, lying on the ground in the woods in the middle of the night, I would have run over immediately. But Killian wasn't me, and Ciaran wasn't anything like my real father, so instead Killian just gaped at him.

"What's happened, then?" he asked.

"Amyranth has been casting dark wave spells," I said tonelessly. "Ciaran wanted me to join him and Amyranth. I said no. So he decided to bring the dark wave on Kithic. I met him here tonight, and then a group of five witches stripped him of his powers."

Killian's eyes widened almost comically. He couldn't even think of what to ask or say, just kept looking from to Hunter to Ciaran in astonishment.

"No," he finally said, all traces of alcohol gone from his voice. "He has no powers? Are you sure?"

"We're sure," Hunter said, not sounding proud about it.

"You stripped Da of his powers. Ciaran MacEwan."

I understood why he was having a hard time with it. Ciaran seemed invincible—unless you knew his true name.

"Can you please take him to a safe place until he's better?" I asked.

Killian still seemed unsure whether or not this was reality. "Aye," he said hesitantly. "Aye. I know a place."

"I'll help you get him to your car," said Hunter. "Watch him closely. He'll be very weak for a while, but when he's able to move, he might . . . hurt himself."

"Aye," said Killian, slowly absorbing the meaning of Hunter's words. He gave me a quick backward glance, then walked over to the father he had feared and respected. Alyce edged back to give him room. Killian put a hand on Ciaran's shoulder and flinched when he saw Ciaran's face. I looked away. Then Hunter and Killian walked away through the woods, supporting Ciaran between them.

Alyce got up slowly and came to sit by me. "It was a hard thing, my dear," she said.

"It hurts," I said inadequately.

"It needs to hurt, Morgan," she said gently, rubbing my back. "If you had done this without it hurting, you would be a monster."

Like Ciaran, I thought. Hunter came back, alone. Alyce kissed my cheek and left, going back through the woods the way she had come. With only Hunter as my witness, I let go and began to cry. He sat down next to me and put his arms around me, hard and familiar. I leaned against him and sobbed until I thought I would make myself sick. And still there was pain inside.

"Morgan, Morgan," Hunter barely murmured. "I love you. I love you. It will be all right."

I had no idea how he could say that.

12.
Alisa

><"It's a thin line between light and dark, between pain and pleasure, between heat and cold, between love and hate, between life and death, between this world and the next."

—Folk saying><

By five o'clock in the morning, I was totally ready to freak. Where the hell had Hunter and his father gone? Why weren't they back? It was going to be dawn soon, and I was supposed to be home! Any minute now, Hilary would be getting up for her sunrise yoga. Eventually she would notice I wasn't at home.

I was stalking around their house, too worried and upset to be tired, though my body felt like I'd been up for days. Should I call a taxi? Wait—this was Widow's Vale. There was no taxi service at five in the morning. I would have to wake someone up to come get me. This sucked!

I was trying to decide if I should just start walking when I heard heavy footsteps on the front porch. I almost flew to the door, just in time to see Hunter and Mr. Niall came in. They looked like someone had taken all the blood out of them while they were out.

"Are you okay?" I blurted. "What's wrong? Where were you?"

Hunter nodded, then patted his father on the back as Mr. Niall passed us, then headed slowly upstairs, his tread lifeless. "I'm sorry, Alisa," Hunter said. "I had no idea it would take so long. Do you need to get home?"

"Yes—but what's happened? Are you okay?"

"I'm all right. Morgan's waiting outside—she'll give you a ride."

"Morgan?"

He nodded, rubbing his hands over his face, pressing gently on his eyes. "Yes. Tonight Morgan met Ciaran MacEwan—we told you about him—out at the power sink. You know, that old Methodist cemetery at the edge of town. Things got strange, and then Morgan ended up putting a binding spell on him. She called me and my da, and we went out there, and we got some other witches, and we stripped Ciaran of his powers."

I stared at him. "You just stripped Ciaran of his powers? Just now?"

"Yes. It was very hard—Ciaran was incredibly powerful, and he resisted strongly. It was especially hard on Morgan."

I could hardly take it all in. "What does this mean about the dark wave?"

Hunter gave a wry smile, and I could tell all he wanted to do was drop onto his bed and sleep for a year. "I would guess there won't be a dark wave now," he said. "Looks like you're off the hook—you won't have to torture yourself with this spell anymore."

It took a moment for the words to sink in. "I can't believe it's all over," I said, getting into my coat. I had been working so hard—we all had. And it had been for nothing. I mean, I was glad there wouldn't be a dark wave coming, but at the same time, in a way I had been almost looking forward to seeing how well I did. Call me self-centered.

My adrenaline started to ebb, and suddenly I could hardly lift my feet enough to walk to the door. I looked back at Hunter, drawn and pale in the harsh overhead light of the living room. "Was it very bad?"

He nodded and looked down at the scarred wooden floor. "It was very bad."

"I'll talk to you soon," I said softly. "Take care of yourself." I gently closed the door behind me and walked across the front porch and out to the street, where Morgan was waiting in her big old car. Hunter and his father had looked awful. I wished there was something I could do for them. Maybe later today I would try to bring them something. What would be good in this situation? Chicken soup?

The door was unlocked and the engine still running when I got in. I looked over at Morgan. "Hi," I said quietly. "It sounds like you guys had a really hard time."

She inclined her head a tiny bit, then put the car into gear and pulled away from the curb. I sneaked another glance at her. Morgan usually looked pretty natural, not too spiffed up, but tonight she looked terrible. Like she had literally been through hell.

"I'm sorry, Morgan," I said. "I'm sorry tonight was so hard, and I'm sorry for how I've acted toward you the past couple of months. I wish—I wish I could help you somehow."

She looked over at me, a pale slash from a streetlight bisecting her face. The edges of her mouth curved in a tiny acknowledgment, and then we turned the corner onto my street. She stopped a few houses away and looked at me expectantly, like she was waiting for me to get out. "Um, should I get out here?" I asked, grabbing my purse.

Morgan nodded. "So your dad doesn't hear the car."

"Ohhh." Very wise, I thought. "You're good at this," I said in admiration, and she let out a little laugh that sounded like broken glass.

I opened the door as quietly as I could and stepped out onto the silent street. When I turned back to whisper thanks, I saw that Morgan's face was shiny with tear tracks. "I'm sorry," I whispered. It was all I could think to say. She gave a small nod and put the car back into drive. Very slowly, she turned around and headed back toward her house.

The morning air was still and heavy as I walked over to my house. It was that last moment of quiet before the early risers get up; I felt like I could breathe in the peaceful sleep of my family and my neighbors and the whole town. After silently making my way to my room, I kicked off my shoes and looked for just a minute out the window. The rim of the horizon was just barely highlighted with pink: the dawn of a new day.

I woke up later that same morning, not even caring how late I was for school. When I went downstairs Hilary looked up in surprise from the yoga mat she had spread on the living-room floor. She glanced at the mantel clock, then looked thoughtful.

"It's Friday, isn't it?" she said. "Aren't you supposed to be in school?"

"Yeah," I said wearily, collapsing on the couch.

"Are you sick again, or did you and your friend stay up too late talking on the phone?"

"I'm sick again."

She uncoiled herself and came to look at me. She wasn't wearing makeup, and somehow she looked both younger and older than twenty-five. I wondered what it was that made my dad so crazy about her. Reaching out, she pressed her hand against my forehead.

"Hm. Well, I guess I should call the school."

"Thanks," I said, not having expected her cooperation. It had never occurred to me that my twenty-five-year-old stepmother-to-be would actually have the authority to do stuff like this.

"Why don't you go back upstairs and get into bed? Do you need anything?"

"No thanks." I hauled myself up and headed to my room as I heard her dialing the school's number.

When I woke up again later, I heard light footsteps in the hall. Hilary tapped on my door and opened it. "Are you awake?"

"Uh-huh." The open eyes are always a good clue.

"It's past lunch. Are you hungry?"

I thought. "Uh-huh."

"Come on downstairs and I'll fix you some nice sardines on crackers," she said, and I stared at her in horror before I noticed she had an evil grin on her face.

I couldn't help smiling back. "Good one."

In the kitchen I fixed myself a PB & J, poured some juice, and sat down.

Hilary sat down across from me. I sighed but tried to hide it behind the sandwich. As much as I didn't want to admit it, she was going to be part of my life. And so was my half sibling. So I should probably make an effort to get along better. I should also ask my doctor for a prescription for Prozac. That could help.

"How's school going?" she asked, destroying all my good intentions.

I looked at her matter-of-factly. "It's high school. It sucks." I waited for her to tell me about how it had been the most wonderful four years of her life, how she was captain of the pep squad—

"Yeah. Mine sucked, too," she said, and my mouth dropped open. "I hated it. I thought it was so stupid and pointless. I mean, I liked a couple of classes, when I had good teachers. And I liked seeing my friends. But you couldn't pay me to go back. It didn't seem to have anything to do with real life."

She was warming to her topic. I stared at this new Hilary in fascination, chewing my sandwich.

"You know what real life is?" she went on. "Knowing how to make change from a dollar. Knowing that virtually everything is alphabetized. That's real life."

"What about mortgages, life insurance, lawn care?" I asked.

"You pick that stuff up as you go along. They don't teach that in school, anyway. Now, college was different, I have to say. College was cool. You could control what you wanted to study and when. You could decide to go to class or not, and no one would hassle you. I looooved college. I took tons of lit and art courses, and fun stuff like women's studies and comparative religion."

"What did you graduate with?"

"A basic liberal arts degree, a bachelor's. Nothing useful for a job or anything." She laughed. "It would have been better if I had studied to be an accountant." She put her arms over her head and stretched. "Which is why I'm doing medical transcription from home. It requires knowing how to listen, read, and type. And I can set my own hours, and the money isn't bad, and I'll be able to do it after the baby's born."

"Is that what you're doing on the computer all the time?" I had thought she was writing a romance novel or having an Internet relationship or something.

"Yeah. Which reminds me. I need to get back to it. Right after *Life and Love*. Want to watch?"

"Okay." I felt compelled to follow this new, body-snatched Hilary. I wondered what they had done with the real Hilary and decided it didn't matter. We sat on the couch in the family room together and she filled me in on her favorite soap.

I watched it mindlessly, enjoying having an hour from my life gone, an hour in which I didn't have to think about magick and witches and breaking things and dark waves. I looked around the house, at Hilary, thought about my dad coming home. His face always lit up when he saw me and Hilary. That was cool. Thank God they weren't going to get wiped out by magick anytime soon.

13.
Morgan

><"The thing about magick is: sometimes it looks like one thing, but it turns out to be something quite different."

—Saffy Reese, New York, 2001><

I slept all day but awoke at five in the afternoon, feeling just as crappy as when I'd gone to sleep. I heard Mary K. coming through the bathroom door and sat up to see her.

"Are you all right?" she asked, looking concerned. "Have you been in bed all day?"

I nodded. "I think I'll get up and take a shower now."

"Is this the flu or what? Alisa was out sick today, too."

"I guess it's just some bug that's going around," I said lamely. I didn't know what Alisa had told my sister, if anything, and didn't want to blow it for her.

"Well, come downstairs if you want dinner. It's little steaks and baked potatoes. And Aunt Eileen and Paula are coming."

I nodded, then pushed my way into the bathroom and shut both doors. I felt heavy and unrested, the knowledge of what I had done the night before weighing me down. My family was having one of my favorite meals, and I always loved seeing my aunt and her girlfriend. But right now the thought of food made my stomach roil, and I didn't feel up to talking to anyone. Maybe I would just go back to bed after my shower.

I made the water as hot as I could stand it and let it rain down on my neck and shoulders. Quietly I started to cry, leaning against the shower wall, my eyes closed against the splashing water. Oh, Goddess, I thought. Goddess. Get me through this. What did I do?

I saved my family, my friends, my coven.

At the expense of my father.

I had seen Ciaran after the rite. He looked dead. And I knew him well enough to know that living without magick would surely drive him insane. I had heard that a witch living without magick was like a person living a half existence, in a world where colors were grayed, scents were dulled, taste was almost nonexistent. Where your hands felt covered by plastic gloves, so when you touched things, you couldn't feel their texture, their vibrations.

That was what I had done to my father last night.

He killed your mother. He's killed hundreds of people, witches and humans. Woman, man, and child. Just like Hunter said.

I doubted that Ciaran would be alive for long. As far as I knew, there was no rite to give him his magick back—it had been ripped from him forever. And without magick, I doubted Ciaran would feel that life was worth living.

Now he was virtually harmless, and the dark wave wasn't

going to come. Not this time. I hoped I would start feeling better soon, either physically or emotionally. I would take either one. My mind was bleeding with pain and guilt and relief, and my body felt like I had fallen on rocks, again and again and again.

After my shower, I got back into bed.

It wasn't long before Mom came upstairs. She sat carefully on the side of my bed and felt my forehead. "You don't feel hot, but you certainly look sick."

"Thanks."

"Does your stomach hurt?"

"No." Just my psyche.

"Okay. How about I fix you a little tray and bring it up?"

I nodded, trying not to cry. Mom was still in her work clothes, and she looked tired. I was almost an adult, seventeen years old, yet all I wanted right now was for my mom to take care of me, to keep me safe. I never wanted to get out of this bed or leave this house again.

After Mom left, Aunt Eileen and Paula came in. Paula had completely recovered from her nasty ice-skating accident and was back at work.

"Big test today?" Aunt Eileen inquired with a smile.

"O ye of little faith."

Paula came over and felt my nose. "You're fine."

"Ha ha." She's a vet.

"You look like death warmed over, honey," said my favorite aunt. "You need anything? Can we bring you something?"

I shook my head, and then Mom was back with my tray. I looked at the food. It was all cut up into little pieces, and I started to cry.

*　　*　　*

"Morgan, can you talk on the phone?" Mary K. asked an hour later. "It's Hunter."

I nodded, and she brought the cordless phone in and gave it to me.

"Hello, my love," he said, and my heart hurt. "How are you doing?"

"Not great. How are you?"

"Bloody awful. Did you get any sleep today?"

"I slept, but it didn't help."

There were a few moments of silence, and I knew what was coming.

"Morgan—I wish you had told me you knew his true name. I thought we trusted each other."

Unexpectedly I felt a little spark of irritation. "If you're pissed, say you're pissed. Don't try to make me feel guilty about my decisions."

"I'm not trying to make you feel guilty," he said more strongly. "I just thought we had total trust and honesty between us."

"The way I trusted you when you were in Canada?"

Long silence. "I guess we have a ways to go."

"I guess we do." I felt upset at what that implied, for both of us.

"Well, I want to work to get there," he said, surprising me. "I want us to grow closer, to earn each other's trust, to be able to count on each other more than we count on other people. I *do* want us to have total trust and honesty between us. That's how I want us to be."

You are perfection, I thought, calming right down. "I'd like that, too."

For a moment I just basked in the glow of having Hunter. "It was just—he's my father. I was probably the only person in the whole world who knew his true name, except him. And he knew I had it. I felt I had to keep it close to myself, in case I ever needed it, for me or for you. Not for the council."

"He knew that you had his true name?"

"He must have. I used it the night we—shape-shifted, to stop him. That's why he disappeared, when what he really wanted to do was kill you or me or both."

"Yet he met you at the power sink."

"I guess he trusted me or was sure he was stronger than me." I gave a brittle laugh. "He *was* stronger than me. Many times stronger than me. But he shouldn't have trusted me." Hot tears slipped from my eyes and rolled down my cheeks.

"Morgan, you know you did the right thing—not only for you, me, and the others he would have hurt, but also for Ciaran. For every evil he did, three times that was coming back to him. You've prevented him from making that any worse."

"That's one way of looking at it," I said. "I don't know. Nothing is ever black or white. Decisions are never crystal clear."

"No. What you did last night was not one hundred percent good, but certainly not one hundred percent bad. But on the whole it was much more good than bad. On the whole, you honored the Goddess much more than you dishonored her. And that's sometimes as much as we can hope for."

"I wish I could see you," I said, feeling his soothing words taking away some of my jagged edges. "But I'm a wreck, and I'm sure Mom wouldn't let me out after I've been in bed all day."

"You just rest up," Hunter said. "We can get together tomorrow. I'd like to get away from here, if possible—my da's driving me mad. He's going mental because I don't want to have anything to do with the council anymore."

"What? What do you mean?"

"I don't trust them anymore. I can't put my faith in them. I can't do as they ask simply because they ask. I can't turn to them for protection. Not only are they no use to me, they've actually been dangerous for me. And for you. And for Da, though he doesn't see it that way."

"Can you quit being a Seeker? Is that allowed?"

Hunter gave a short laugh. "It doesn't happen frequently, that's certain. I haven't talked to anyone officially about it yet—Da's still trying to talk me out of it. But in my heart I know this is what I want to do."

I was stunned. Hunter's dissatisfaction with the council had been building for a while, but it had never occurred to me that he would quit being a Seeker. It was what he was; it was a huge part of what defined him.

"Whoa," I said. "If you're not a Seeker, what will you do?"

"I don't know," he admitted. "I've never done anything else, and no one besides the council needs a Seeker. I'll have to think about it. But how do *you* feel about it, my quitting?"

"I think you should do whatever you feel like you need to do," I said. "You could do anything you want. I'll help you do anything you want."

"Oh, Morgan, that means so much to me," he said, sounding relieved. "You have no idea. If you'll support me, I'll take on anyone." He paused. "They're not going to want me to quit," he explained.

"I know. Let's talk about it tomorrow, in person," I said. "This could be good. This could be very exciting. I want to look toward the future instead of dreading everything in the present."

"I'm with you there," Hunter said. "Now I guess I'll go try to avoid Da. Goddess, fathers can be a pain in the arse."

"Yes, they can," I said with dry irony.

"See you tomorrow, my love."

"Tomorrow."

"Morgan, maybe you would feel better if you ate an actual breakfast," said Mary K., sitting across from me at the kitchen table.

I looked up, bleary-eyed. It was starting to seem that maybe I really did have the flu. I still felt awful, with bone-deep aches, a pounding headache, and lingering nausea. I had staggered down to the kitchen, grabbed a regular Coke for its medicinal properties, and now felt a tiny bit better.

"It's settling my stomach."

"There's some oatmeal left. It's got raisins in it." Mary K. took a healthy bite of her banana and gave me a perky, bright-eyed look. That was how she was. She wasn't even trying to be this way. This morning, even though she hadn't taken a shower yet, she looked fresh and clean, with perfect skin and shiny hair. I hadn't taken a shower, either, and I could scare small children.

"No, thank you. Where are Mom and Dad?"

"Dad's downstairs, rebuilding his motherboard. Mom had to show some houses. And I am going to Jaycee's, as soon as you give me a ride." She gave me a simpering smile and batted her eyelashes at me, and I couldn't help laughing.

"Okay. Let me get a grip."

*   *   *

An hour later I dropped her at Jaycee's house, then swung around and headed for Hunter's. The shower had helped, and then I had taken three Tylenol. Now I'd had a second Coke and a piece of toast here in the car, and I hoped that something I'd done would start to help soon.

It was better, though, walking up to Hunter's front door without feeling like I had to be looking over my shoulder. I had no idea whether Amyranth would take up Ciaran's cause, but I had the feeling that this had been a purely personal thing. I might not matter to them at all.

The front door opened. "Hi," said Hunter.

I blinked when I saw him. "Do you still feel bad? You look awful."

He rubbed his hand over his unshaven jaw. Unlike the hair on his head, which was the color of sunlight, his beard was dark, and so was his chest hair. Which I was going to stop thinking about immediately.

He shrugged and I went past him, automatically heading for the fireplace in the living room. I dropped my coat and sank onto the couch, stretching my feet toward the flames. The house smelled pleasantly smoky, clean. Fire has great purifying qualities.

"I think I feel better than I did yesterday," he said, sitting next to me so our legs touched. "Maybe it just takes a while. I've never been around a dark wave before, so I don't know."

I leaned my head against his shoulder and shivered at the warmth I found there. "Maybe you haven't drunk enough tea," I said with a straight face.

"Quite the wit, aren't you?" He put his arms around me and we snuggled, taking comfort from being close.

"Where's your dad?" Please be out of the house. Please be gone all day.

"Getting groceries. There's nothing to eat because we've been kind of busy the last few days."

I pushed against Hunter's shoulder so he would fall sideways. "Perfect."

"Good idea," he said, sliding down and pulling me with him. Then we were lying on the couch, face-to-face, pressed together, and my entire back was toasting nicely from the fire.

Simultaneously we both made happy sounds, then laughed at ourselves. I didn't feel like making out, sadly enough, and neither did he, and instead we just held each other close, snuggling hard, feeling some of our aches disappear with the heat from each other's body. Goddess, if I could just lie like this forever. Hunter's hand stroked my back absently; our eyes were closed, and I had my arms around his waist, not even caring that one was getting smushed.

"Thursday was so awful," I murmured against his chest. "I don't think I'll ever get over it. No matter how much good I was doing, I still know I betrayed my father. And despite how bad he was, there was something in him that I felt I knew, something good, from long ago. That was the part of him I liked."

"I understand." Hunter's warm breath stirred my hair. "The only thing that will make you feel better is time. Give yourself time. I promise there will be a day when it doesn't hurt so much."

I felt tears behind my eyelids but didn't let them out. I was tired of crying, of being in pain. I wanted to lie here and feel safe and loved and warm.

"Mmm," I hummed, moving closer to him. "This feels so great. I needed this."

It wasn't long until we felt Hunter's father come home, and we sat up as if we had been discussing the weather the whole time. I'm sure Mr. Niall was fooled.

Hunter helped him carry the groceries into the kitchen. When I saw Mr. Niall's face, I thought he looked even older and grayer than usual, which was saying something. However, when he saw me, he actually nodded and said, "Hullo, Morgan. Hope you're feeling better." So he had softened up to me. Maybe I should write an article for a teen magazine about how to win over your boyfriend's parents. But I guess most girls wouldn't have my same setup.

"What's in here, Da?" Hunter said, his arms full. "This weighs a ton."

"I thought you were supposed to be so *strong*," said Mr. Niall snidely, and my eyebrows went up.

"I am strong; I just don't know why they sell lead weights at the grocery store, that's all."

Their bickering continued as they went into the kitchen, and it was still going on when they came out. I frowned, thinking. Then I glanced at the potted winter cactus by the window. It had been blooming last week. Now it was dead. My heart sank, and a cold feeling came over me. Oh, no. Oh, no. I stood up and went over to them, looking closely at their faces.

"What, Morgan?" Hunter asked.

"I—we all feel horrible. You guys are arguing. That plant is dead." I was too upset to make sense, but it took them only a moment to get it.

"Oh, Goddess," Hunter breathed.

"Of course." Mr. Niall shook his head. "I knew something was wrong—I just couldn't see what. But you're right. I know you are."

Hunter muttered a word that I was never allowed to use. "Too right," he said. "The dark wave is still coming. Either Ciaran cast it before he came to see you, or Amyranth is continuing his work without him."

"Call Alisa," said Mr. Niall grimly.

14.
Alisa

><"I see one day when all witches everywhere are united in one common doctrine, one common cause. I see Woodbanes everywhere safe from prejudice. I see our detractors, our persecutors, our enemies, a threat no longer. I see one great clan, not seven, with all the members of that clan Woodbane brothers and sisters. This is my vision, the one I am working toward."

—X, an Amyranth leader, London, 2002><

It seemed that every time I looked out a window, it was darker outside, more ominous. Mr. Niall had turned on the radio in the kitchen, and every once in a while we heard faint weather reports about a bad early-spring storm coming, how unusual it was. They joked about how it was March, still roaring in like a lion, ha ha. It had all seemed so unreal. How could the world be going on as usual when I knew that mine might end at any minute?

Concentrate, I told myself. Concentrate. Okay, third form: spell specifics. This was difficult—not as hard as the second part, but harder than the first or fourth. Facing east, I began to step in the carefully designed pattern that would help define and clarify this spell. Next to me, as if we were in pairs skating, Mr. Niall started the same motions.

"Words," Hunter muttered. He and Morgan were sitting on the floor, their backs against the wall. It had been almost six hours ago that Hunter had called me and told me the dark wave was still coming. Since then I had been struggling to understand: What? Coming? Now? It was hard to get my head around the dark wave again, and there almost wasn't time, with all the practice we were doing. It was like a strange, nightmare day, like I would wake up any minute safe in my bed. But deep in my witch bones I knew that wouldn't happen.

Morgan had her head on her knees, as if she were too miserable to move. Hunter looked like he'd been run over by a truck. Mr. Niall had a washcloth, and he kept patting his forehead with it. He looked gray and clammy and had to sit down every few minutes.

"Oh, right," I said. I rubbed my aching temples with my hands and wished I had something to drink. "Nogac haill, bets carrein, hest farrill, mai nal nithrac, boc maigeer." I said the ancient words, whose meanings I knew only very sketchily, as I stepped again in the pattern I'd been taught. My hands drew patterns of sigils and runes in the air as I described exactly what we needed this spell to do, how and when and why. The third part usually took about seventeen minutes if I did it properly.

"No—arms up," Mr. Niall croaked.

His interruption broke my concentration; my foot faltered, and all at once I fell out of sync, with no idea of where I was supposed to be in the spell. I stared at my arms, which were not up, and then a wave of tiredness and nausea swept over me.

"You're doing great, Alisa," said Hunter as I stood there dejectedly, rubbing my forehead. His voice sounded stiff and leaden, as if even talking made him feel worse. "It's just an incredibly difficult spell. It would take *me* a solid month to learn it."

"Yeah, but you would understand what the hell you were doing and saying and why. I'm just memorizing it like a parrot."

"A talented parrot," Morgan said, trying to smile.

Mr. Niall slowly lowered himself to the wooden floor and curled up there with a moan. He looked like someone had taken all his stuffing out and returned the pelt. Of the four of us, he seemed the worst off. I glanced at Hunter and met his eyes: We both knew there was no way Daniel could even pretend to cast this spell himself. I'd been here three hours, and in that short time I'd watched as the three full blood witches visibly deteriorated. Even I was starting to feel pretty bad—my headache made it hard to concentrate, and my knees felt shaky.

"I'll go make tea," said Morgan, and she carefully uncurled herself and went into the kitchen.

Hunter got up to stand next to me. "It's going to be up to you," he said, so his father couldn't hear, and I nodded, wishing I were in Florida and this were all their problem.

"I know," I whispered back. "But I'm not ready, Hunter— you know it. What if when the time comes, I can't do it? I mean, I'm trying hard, but—" My voice wobbled and broke, and I wiped a hand across my stinging eyes. I refused to cry and look like a baby in front of him.

Morgan came back with a tray of mugs. She knelt on the floor by Mr. Niall, sloshing the tea a bit. "Here," she told him. "Drink this."

He pushed himself up with effort and stretched a bony hand toward the mug. "Ta, lass."

Hunter and I sat on the floor. I was incredibly thirsty and

sucked down some of the hot, sweet tea. Morgan had put extra sugar and lemon in it, and it tasted great.

"The wave is coming," Hunter said baldly, and I saw Morgan flinch. "Alisa has done an amazing job of learning the spell as much as she can, but she's not quite ready. No one could be."

"I'll do it," said Mr. Niall.

"There's no way you could do it, Da," Hunter said. "You know it and I know it. The wave has already made you so weak, I'll have to practically carry you to the car, anyway."

"You couldn't carry—" Mr. Niall began, showing a spark of life.

"Please." Morgan held up her hand. "Could we not waste time? What are we going to *do*?"

"I think I might have an idea," Hunter said slowly.

"This is going to feel terrible," Hunter warned me. My hair was whipping around in the wind, as was Morgan's. She quickly stuffed hers down the back of her coat, and I did the same. Here in the old Methodist cemetery the air felt weird, like it had an actual weight that was pressing down on us—humid but cold. We were standing before the power sink, listening as Hunter explained his big idea. Mr. Niall's head was bowed, and he was bent over on himself.

"What do you call it again?" I asked.

Hunter smiled wanly. "A tàth meànma."

I frowned, still confused. "And why can't I just connect—or whatever—with Mr. Niall?"

Hunter cast a glance at his father, who appeared to be in too much pain to be paying much attention. "Because my da isn't strong enough," he said quietly. "He doesn't have enough power right now to connect with you and still stay a safe distance from the dark wave. Morgan has enough power for both of them, essentially, and she'll be able to hold you two together." He looked at me. "Make sense?"

I nodded. "And, um . . . why will it hurt?" Not that it mattered.

Morgan smiled weakly. "Before you do a tàth meànma like this, it's best to do purification rituals, fast, drink herbal tea, and so on," she explained. "For a little tàth meànma, it doesn't matter so much. For one like this, it would have been better. It's going to feel bad for me, too." She made a pained expression.

"Great." I smiled wanly. "And where will you be?"

"The field across the road, on the other side of the woods. I'll be close enough to keep contact, but I hope not close enough to get hit."

A sudden sob rose in my throat and I pressed my lips together hard. Sure, we were going to try Hunter's big idea, but in the end it was up to me, and I'm not hero material by any stretch of the imagination. I had worked as hard as I knew how, I would try my best, but my best just might not be good enough. The truth was, if I didn't come through, we had all gathered out here to die. I wouldn't have to be a flower girl for Hilary after all.

"Okay," I said, trying to sound somewhat less terrified than I was.

"And Daniel will be farther away than that, on the other side of Morgan," Hunter explained. "He can keep in touch with Morgan, and Morgan will keep in touch with you, and we'll do this thing. Right?"

"Right," I said, not meaning it. This was Hunter's idea· I

would still perform the spell, but my mind would be linked with Morgan's. Her mind would be linked with Mr. Niall's, and he would feed her lines if necessary that she could pass on to me. Hunter was going to stay here at the power sink with me, watching my movements and coaching me. He knew what to look for, even if he couldn't do it himself.

A chill wind smacked my face at that moment. I looked up, and on the far horizon was a hovering cloud of what looked like fine ash. It was roiling, boiling, rolling toward Widow's Vale, like an impossibly large swarm of insects.

Hunter glanced up at the sky, then at his dad, who seemed to be crumpling. "Right, everyone. Let's get going. It's on its way."

Morgan, looking pale and tense, stood facing me. We put our hands on each other's shoulders. Slowly we came together, so that our foreheads touched. Morgan's was icy cold and clammy. We both had long hair, and now the angry wind twisted the strands together around our heads. I was dimly aware of Hunter and Mr. Niall leaving, and I knew Hunter would be back. Then I shut my eyes and concentrated, the way they had told me to do. Basically I was supposed to meditate and clear my mind and let Morgan do all the heavy lifting.

I stood there, the wind creeping under my coat like icicles, and wondered when this was all going to get started. Then my consciousness seemed to wink, and I felt a fine, pointed pain, as if a metal claw were clamping down on my skull. Just as I was starting to think I couldn't stand any more of this, Morgan was there, in my mind.

"Relax," her voice came to me, though I knew my ears weren't hearing it. "Let everything go. In this moment, you are safe and everything is perfect. Let everything relax. Take down your walls, and let me in."

"It hurts," I said, feeling like a sissy.

"I know," Morgan said. "I feel it, too. We have to let go of it."

I thought about taking down walls, and slowly I realized that Morgan and I were somehow joined—I could see inside her, and she could see inside me: we were one person. I felt an unexpected elation—this was beautiful, magickal, exciting. It was a glow of golden light, surrounded by a corona of finely etched pain. I thought of what the moon's shadow looked like as it moved across the sun.

Then I followed Morgan deeper into her mind. There I saw all her knowledge of magick, her feelings for Hunter, all this stuff about Ciaran—I felt Morgan deliberately leading me away from her personal thoughts.

"Focus," came her voice, gentle and strong. "I'm going to leave now, but we'll stay joined. Soon you'll feel just a bit of Mr. Niall. We'll stay with you the whole time. You will be able to do this. You have all the support you need. You're a strong, beautiful witch, and with this one act, one spell, you will set your life on an exhilarating path."

This wasn't how Morgan usually talked, but I had the feeling it was who she really was, inside. On the outside she was kind of shy and hard to get to know. Inside, she was glowing and powerful and ancient.

"Focus," came her voice.

Slowly I opened my eyes, feeling nausea trying to take over. I clamped it down and tried to forget about it. Outside, it was almost as dark as night. What little light there was looked strange, tinted with an almost greenish hue, as if right before an eclipse. Bits of last year's leaves were whipping around, swirling in tiny dust devils on top of headstones. Feeling dreamy, relaxed, and stupidly confident, I saw Hunter coming back through the woods. I felt Morgan's awareness of him through my eyes, felt her rush of love, of longing, of uncertainty. I tried not to pay attention to it.

Hunter's eyes looked huge and green, with dark hollows beneath them. His face was white and looked carved out of marble, his cheekbones angled sharply, the skin stretched tight.

"Begin," he said.

It was an incredibly weird feeling, being connected to Morgan. As long as I didn't think about it, I was okay. Whenever I remembered it again, I felt a rush of pain and nausea. Hunter handed me a large bowl of salt, and with this I traced a circle of protection on the ground. He helped by placing stones of power and protection all around that circle. Then I buried my hands in the salt and rubbed it against my skin. The rest I sprinkled around me. I had four embossed silver bowls that Hunter had given me. In one was dirt, in another water. In one was a tiny fire that Morgan had kindled, so it wasn't affected by the wind, and in the last was incense burning with an orange glow. I put these cups at east, south, west, and north to represent the four elements. Mr. Niall had given me a gold pocket watch, and I set that in the center of my circle. Then I was ready to begin the first part. It should take almost twenty minutes, if I did it correctly.

Just as I raised my arms, I felt a shimmering presence: Mr. Niall. In my mind he was called Maghach, but Morgan was just called Morgan. After a moment to get used to this new presence, I took a deep, cleansing breath, released it, and began.

"On this day, at this hour, I invoke the Goddess and the God," I said, holding my arms skyward. "You who are pure in your intent, aid me in this spell. By earth and water and fire and air, strengthen this spell. By spring and summer and fall and winter, strengthen this spell. By witches both past and present, of my blood and not of my blood, strengthen this spell. Help my heart be pure, my crafting joyous, my hands sure and steady, and my mind open to receive your wisdom."

Here I drew runes and sigils to identify myself as the spell-worker and Mr. Niall as the spellcrafter. I identified the place, the time of year, the phase of the moon, the hour of the day. Then I walked deasil in a circle three times, my arms held out.

> *"I make this spell to right a wrong,*
> *I need your help to make it strong.*
> *Today we join to heal a wound,*
> *My voice will lift in joyous sound.*
> *My hope is ancient, vision sure;*
> *The goal I seek is good and pure.*
> *I am your servant, I ask again,*
> *Show faith in magick, ease our pain."*

After this came a simple power chant, designed to raise whatever powers I had as well as to call the Goddess and the God. Whenever I had practiced this at Hunter's, I'd caused something to explode, so I wasn't sure what would happen now.

Morgan's voice came to me in my head. *Alisa, you're doing so well.*

I drew more sigils in the air and on the ground. Mr. Niall had explained these as being a kind of history, quickly describing who he was and who I was and whatever we knew about the power sink. Then I knelt back down. The first part was done.

I heard Morgan say that the first part had been perfect and to go into the second part. I stood up and took another breath, holding my arms out to my sides. I was aware of a cold, damp wind whipping my hair around, I knew that it was pitch-dark outside, but mostly I was aware within myself of the perfect, lovely form of the spell that Maghach had crafted. In my mind I could it see it all finished, done, its layers upon layers. I needed to focus and do it step by step.

The second part was the longest and hardest. Something in me started to feel anxious, as if I were running out of time. It was either Morgan or Maghach. I stepped quickly into the form of the second part, the limitations.

"This spell is to ignite on the thirtieth day of the first month of spring," I began, my voice sounding thin against the wind. "The moon is full and on the wane. The length of the spell shall not exceed five minutes after igniting. It shall be contained within these barriers."

Here I knelt and drew sigils on the ground, then runes that further identified the exact location, to within a hundred feet, of where the spell would have life. I began to feel an urgency, and I drew more quickly. Suddenly my mind went blank, and I stared down at the ground and my unmoving hand. Another sigil? Another rune? On the ground? In the air? Do I get up now? An icy bead of sweat trickled down my back as adrenaline flooded my body. *Oh no oh no oh no.*

"Tyr," came Morgan's voice, calm and sure inside my head. I almost started weeping with relief. I drew the rune tyr on the ground with sharp movements. "Ur," she went on patiently. "Thorn. Then yr. Then the battle sigil, in the air."

Yes, yes, I thought, following her instructions.

"Sigils for moon phase," she coached me gently.

Yes, I know now. I thought back, recognizing my place once again. I walked in the circle in the shape of a moon, then drew its identity in the air.

"The spell shall have no other purpose than that described here," I went on. "It shall affect no other being than those described here. It shall not exist or ignite ever again in perpetuity, except for the time described here. This spell is intended only for goodness, for safety, to right a wrong. My intent is pure. I work not in anger, nor hatred, nor judgment."

On and on I went. The limitations of a spell are the most important part, especially for something like this.

This part took almost thirty minutes. I moved as quickly as I could and still be precise and exact, not skipping anything. Three more times I forgot what to do, and each time panic overwhelmed me until Morgan talked me through the next step. Her voice sounded strained but incredibly calm and reassuring. I was no longer aware of where Hunter was or what he was doing. I felt a dim outline of Maghach in my head. Sometimes I felt cold wind, or a heavy weight pressing on me, or was aware of leaves whipping around me. I stayed within my circle and worked the spell.

At the end of the second part I wanted to lie down and cry. The air itself was starting to feel bad, to affect me as if I were breathing fumes of poison. I felt exhausted and nauseated, and my head pounded. The third part was the actual form of the spell itself. The fourth part would be fast: igniting it.

"Keep going, Alisa," said Morgan, a thin line of ice underlying her calm voice. "Keep going. You can do it. You're strong. You know it. Now state the actual spell."

I wiped the sweat off my forehead and turned to the east. "With this spell I create an opening, a bith dearc, between this world and the netherworld," I began, my voice sounding shaky. "I create an unnatural tear between life and death, between light and dark, between salvation and revenge." And on it went, sometimes in English, sometimes in modern Gaelic, which I had done a decent job of memorizing, and some in ancient Gaelic, which Morgan and Maghach had to coach me through, practically word by word. I walked within my circle, creating patterns, layers of patterns, layers of description, layers of intent. I drew sigils in the air and on the ground. I drew sigils on myself and around myself. Suddenly I froze, looking at the billowing, oily black cloud roaring our way. It looked sickening, tinged with green, and it was getting so close. I felt like the breath was knocked out of me. Oh my God, this was real, and it was here, and I was really going to die. We were all really going to die.

Morgan started talking to me, but I couldn't move. The closer it got, the sicker I felt, and the more Morgan's voice sounded strained and weak. I barely felt Maghach at all anymore.

It's over, I thought. I won't finish in time. I looked around wildly for Hunter and saw him hunched over next to a tombstone. When he looked up at me, he looked like he had aged thirty years.

I had so much more to go, and the black cloud of destruction was almost upon us. Morgan's voice in my head urged me on, and like a robot I started working through the last section of the third part, going as fast as I could. I was shaking all over: I thought I would throw up at any second, and basically I felt like I was standing there waiting to die.

The first blast of death, of darkness, was barely twenty yards away.

My hands trembling, I sketched an inverted pentagram in the air before me. I had finished the third part of the spell.

"Ignite it!" Hunter yelled, his voice sounding strangled.

"Ignite it!" Morgan screamed in my head.

Again I felt frozen with terror, shaky and stupid and ill. The dark wave was almost upon us, and I was mesmerized by it. In its boiling, choking clouds I could see faint outlines of faces, pinched and withered and hungry, eager. My body went cold. Each one of those people had once been someone like me—someone facing this terrible cloud. It was horrifying. The most horrible thing I had ever seen or even imagined.

"Ignite it! Alisa!" Morgan screamed.

Mindless with fear, I mechanically whispered the words that would set the spell into motion, that would let it spark into life, for good or for bad. Shaking so much I could hardly stand, I held out my arms and choked out, "Nal nithrac, cair na rith la, cair nith la!"

I felt a huge surge of energy inside me—it seemed to start in the ground, then it shot through me and out from my fingers and the top of my head. It was warmth and light and energy and happiness all at once: my magickal power. Then the faces were *here*, and the air and the earth ripped open in front of me, as if the whole world as I knew it, reality, were just a painting that someone had slashed. The gold pocket watch I had placed on the ground exploded, and the blast knocked me off my feet. I flew backward and my head cracked against a marble tombstone. Sparks exploded in my throbbing head, and I cried out. Ten feet away, I saw the dark wave suddenly rushing down into the rip, the bith dearc I had made. The ghost faces in it looked surprised, then horrified, then enraged. But they had no power over the spell I had cast. The whole wave disappeared into the rip while I stared. Then my vision went fuzzy, and everything became blessedly quiet and safe, black and still.

"Oh, God," I moaned, trying to feel the back of my head. "Oh, God, this hurts."

"Stay still for a moment," said Morgan's voice.

I blinked up at her. She was sitting next to me, and she seemed to be smashing some greenish moss together in her hands. "My head hurts," I said, like a little kid, and then I remembered everything. "Oh, God!" I cried, trying to sit up, only to be struck down by pain. "Morgan, what happened? What happened?"

When her eyes met mine, I realized that she was no longer inside my mind, but separate and herself. In her eyes I saw so much more than I had ever seen before. It was like a wise, learned woman was inside Morgan's body, and that woman's eyes were telling me things I could only barely begin to understand.

"Morgan?"

"Hold on," she said, then gently lifted my head and pressed her gunk against where it hurt.

"Ow!"

"You'll feel better soon," she said.

A shadow fell across me, and I looked up to see Hunter.

He crouched down next to me, and Morgan nodded as if to tell him I would be all right.

"You did it," Hunter said, his voice sounding raspy. "Alisa, you did it. You performed the spell. It worked. You saved us."

Unexpectedly this made me start crying, which made my head hurt more. Morgan, who I'd always thought of as a little cold, took my hand and patted it, her own eyes shining with tears.

"Morgan did it," I said, trying to stop crying. " I almost forgot everything. She told me what to do."

"Hunter's father told me what to say to you," she said. "It was him. I was just a messenger." She looked wrung out and tired, and there were bits of dried grass and leaves in her hair.

Very slowly I sat up and found that the horrible throbbing in my head had lessened. "Where is Mr. Niall?" I asked. "I don't feel him anymore."

"Right there." Hunter pointed. About fifteen feet away, Hunter's father was kneeling on the ground. "He's closing the bith dearc forever," Hunter explained. "Only this one, of course. There will always be more, and other dark waves, too. But as far as we know, this is the first and only time anyone's ever defeated one. Now we can teach others how to do it. By this time next year maybe we'll have put a stop to Amyranth for good."

Morgan fished in her coat and found a purple scarf, which she tied over my head. "When you get home, leave that stuff on for another two hours. Then wash your hair," she instructed me. "Then take some Tylenol and pass out. You've earned it."

I looked around. "I can't believe it," I said. "It worked. We're still alive. Everyone's still alive." More tears coursed down my cheeks, and I rubbed them away with my sleeve.

Morgan leaned against Hunter, and he put his arm around her.

"I used my powers," I said in wonder.

"You sure did." A hint of a smile crossed Morgan's face.

We looked at each other for a long moment, and I realized that Morgan and I understood each other. We had bonded. We were witches.

15.
Morgan

><"The Nal Nithrac spell is lengthy and difficult, but not impossible for one witch to perform. While the basic spell can be utilized against any dark wave, care must be taken to make it accurate as to the place, time, and people involved. As was shown in Widow's Vale, it is of great value to have some item that carries the vibrations of the wave creator, but it is not always necessary."
—Daniel Niall of Turloch-eigh><

"I can't believe it's over," said Hunter.

I nodded, smiling weakly. "I just want life to get back to normal—whatever normal is," I said. I stretched my feet toward the fire in Hunter's living room. It had taken us a while to make it back to our cars and figure out if we could drive or not, but now we were resting and drinking hot mulled cider.

"All of you performed magnificently," said Hunter's father.

"We made a great team," said Hunter. Alisa looked pleased. Which reminded me. I got up and checked the back of her head. She'd stopped bleeding an hour ago, and she said it didn't hurt that much anymore. I had given her some arnica montana to take every six hours for two days, and I knew she'd heal pretty quickly.

"I can't wait for other witches to hear about this," I said. "For so long no one's had any defense against a dark wave. Now they do. It's like you discovered penicillin, Mr. Niall."

"Please call me Daniel," he said, "or Maghach."

Thank the Goddess, I thought. He was finally accepting me. Besides, my tongue kept tripping over "Mr. Niall," and we'd already been through a tàth meànma together.

"I'm hopeful that the spell will work in other places, when needed," Daniel said. "As long as the specifications and limitations are adjusted accordingly. But yes, this is wonderful news for the whole witch community."

"I still can't believe what it felt like, when I felt the power flow through me," Alisa said. "It was—really—"

"Indescribable," I said, and she nodded.

"In a good way," she added.

"Good," said Hunter. "Now we have to start teaching you things. But first, I'm starved—I haven't eaten in a week, it seems like."

"I'm hungry, too," said Daniel.

"Pizza would be good," Alisa suggested.

"Yeah, we could—" I stopped and gasped, then looked at the mantel clock. "Oh, no, I am way late!" I said, scrambling to my feet. I still felt like I was recovering from the flu, but I knew I was getting better, and that made it okay. "Mom is going to kill me—this is the second time this week."

When I looked up, three pairs of eyes were watching me with amusement. "What?" I said.

"You just saved all of Kithic," Alisa said, snickering.

"And you're worried about being late for dinner," said Hunter.

"Do you want me to call your parents?" Daniel offered. "I could explain why you were unavoidably delayed."

We all broke into laughter, and I shook my head.

"I really should get home," I said. "But I'll see you guys soon."

I got into my coat, and Hunter walked me out to the front porch.

"Can you make it home okay?" he asked, putting his arms around me, holding me tight.

"Yeah." I snuggled closer. "We really stopped it. We stopped the dark wave."

"Yes, we did." His hand stroked my hair, which I knew still had grass in it.

I looked up at him. "Now we have to look toward the future. Like figuring out what you want to do if you leave the council. And if we're ever going to have time *alone together*," I said meaningfully, and he grinned.

"Yes, we must talk about that soon."

We kissed good-bye, and I walked out to Das Boot. The dark wave was no more. Ciaran was no longer a threat to me or anyone else, and someday I hoped to come to terms with how that had happened. Hunter and I were thinking about our future—together.

When I pulled into my driveway and walked slowly up the path, I felt unnaturally light and free. The humidity and weight were gone from the air. I almost felt like skipping.

Then my gaze fell to the ground beneath me. I knelt down to get a closer look, and when I saw them, I let out a gleeful little laugh.

My mother's crocuses, bright purple and yellow, had miraculously sprung back to life.